A Word from Stephanie
about Best Friends and Boyfriends

I never expected that planning a surprise party could turn into one giant disaster! It all started when Darcy, one of my best friends, asked me to do her a big favor. Darcy just started dating Alex Ames, a very cool, very cute new guy at school. He also happens to be the biggest star on the John Muir track team. And our biggest meet of the year was coming up. Darcy is a total sports nut, and she really wanted to help Alex— and our school—win the meet. So she came up with a brilliant plan.

She decided to run with Alex in the early mornings. She figured the extra practices would give him an edge. Then her mom told her she couldn't get up early *every* day. So Darcy asked me to fill in on her days off. Great idea, right?

Wrong! Because once I started getting to know Alex, something very surprising happened. I was falling for my best friend's boyfriend! Think that isn't a problem? Then it never happened to you! Even my family didn't know how to help me out of this jam. And I have a very big, very smart family.

There are nine people and a dog in my very full house. There's me, my big sister, D.J., my little sister, Michelle, and my dad, Danny. And that's just the beginning.

When my mom died, Dad needed help. So he asked his old college buddy, Joey Gladstone, and my uncle Jesse to come live with us to help take care of me and my sisters.

Back then, Uncle Jesse didn't know much about taking care of three little girls. He was more into rock 'n' roll. Joey didn't know anything about kids, either—but it sure was funny watching him learn.

Having Uncle Jesse and Joey around was like having three dads instead of one! But then something even better happened—Uncle Jesse fell in love. He married Rebecca Donaldson, Dad's co-host on his TV show, *Wake Up, San Francisco*. Aunt Becky's so nice—she's more like a big sister than an aunt.

Next Uncle Jesse and Aunt Becky had twin boys. Their names are Nicky and Alex, and they are adorable!

I love being part of a big family. Still, things can get pretty crazy when you live in such a full house!

FULL HOUSE™: Stephanie novels

Available from MINSTREL Books

For orders other than by individual consumers, Pocket Books grants a discount on the purchase of **10 or more** copies of single titles for special markets or premium use. For further details, please write to the Vice-President of Special Markets, Pocket Books, 1633 Broadway, New York, NY 10019-6785, 8th Floor.

For information on how individual consumers can place orders, please write to Mail Order Department, Simon & Schuster Inc., 200 Old Tappan Road, Old Tappan, NJ 07675.

FULL HOUSE™
Stephanie

Hello Birthday,
Good-bye Friend

Laura O'Neil

A Parachute Book

A MINSTREL® BOOK

Published by POCKET BOOKS
New York   London   Toronto   Sydney   Tokyo   Singapore

The sale of this book without its cover is unauthorized. If you purchased this book without a cover, you should be aware that it was reported to the publisher as "unsold and destroyed." Neither the author nor the publisher has received payment for the sale of this "stripped book."

This book is a work of fiction. Names, characters, places and incidents are products of the author's imagination or are used fictitiously. Any resemblance to actual events or locales or persons living or dead is entirely coincidental.

A MINSTREL PAPERBACK *Original*

A Minstrel Book published by
POCKET BOOKS, a division of Simon & Schuster Inc.
1230 Avenue of the Americas, New York, NY 10020

A PARACHUTE BOOK

Copyright © and ™ 1999 by Warner Bros.

FULL HOUSE, characters, names and all related indicia are trademarks of Warner Bros. © 1999.

All rights reserved, including the right to reproduce this book or portions thereof in any form whatsoever. For information address Pocket Books, 1230 Avenue of the Americas, New York, NY 10020.

ISBN: 0-671-02160-5

First Minstrel Books printing February 1999

10 9 8 7 6 5 4 3 2 1

A MINSTREL BOOK and colophon are registered trademarks of Simon & Schuster Inc.

Cover photo by Schultz Photography

Printed in the U.S.A.

QBP/✖

Hello Birthday, Good-bye Friend

CHAPTER
1

◆ ◀ ✦ ◆

"Darcy is *so* crazy about Alex!" Stephanie Tanner squinted in the afternoon sunlight. She lifted one hand to shade her blue eyes. Across the school yard, her best friend, Darcy Powell, stood talking to a tall, athletic-looking boy.

"Alex is *really* cute," Maura Potter commented. Maura stood next to Stephanie, getting ready to head home. She reached up, pulling her brown curls into a scrunchie. "And a total sports nut."

"So is Darcy," Allie Taylor added.

"Exactly," Stephanie said. "That's why it makes sense. Of course Darcy would be nuts about the new star of the track team."

"But I'm not sure Alex is a nice guy." Allie frowned and shook her head. Her straight reddish-brown hair swung around her thin cheeks. "He seems stuck on himself, if you ask me."

Stephanie raised her eyebrows and gazed at Allie in surprise. Allie was her other best friend. They'd known each other since kindergarten. They both loved reading and music and movies. And they could spend hours chatting on the phone.

In some ways, they were opposites. Allie was quiet and loved taking long walks. Stephanie was outgoing and liked being on the move—skating, jogging, biking. Still, they usually agreed about important things. Like boys.

"Alex is stuck on himself?" Stephanie repeated. "Why do you think that?"

Alex Ames just transferred to John Muir Middle School. No one really knew him well.

"It's just a feeling I have," Allie admitted.

"Why shouldn't he be stuck on himself?" Maura giggled. "He is so incredibly good looking! I love the way his hair waves over his eyes. They're an incredible color. I never saw that shade of brown before."

"Darcy calls them amber," Stephanie said. "She's always talking about them. Though I think she's more impressed by his time on the five-hundred yard dash."

"He's the fastest runner John Muir has ever had," Maura added." He's been on the team only a few months, and already he's ranked number two in our league."

"But sports aren't everything," Allie argued. "You know who I think Darcy should date?"

"Ben Kingston," Stephanie instantly replied. She and Maura grinned at each other.

"How could we *not* know that?" Maura teased Allie. "You only mention it every day."

Allie had recently begun dating a guy named Spencer Loman. Ben was Spencer's best friend. Allie was dying to set up a double date with Ben and Darcy.

"Ben has a huge crush on Darcy," Allie said. "He's a great guy. And he's pretty cute, too. I even told Darcy he liked her—but all she can think about is Alex."

"That's what love does to you." Maura sighed.

"It's not love. It's a dumb crush," Allie answered. "I just wish Darcy would give Ben a chance."

"No way," Stephanie said. She gazed at the track. Alex and Darcy were saying good-bye. They stared into each other's eyes and held hands

3

as if they never wanted to let go. And Alex was just leaving for an hour of track practice!

Stephanie saw Darcy turn and head across the field toward home. "Hey, Darce! Over here!" she called.

Darcy saw her and turned to hurry over. Her black, blunt cut hair glistened in the sunlight as she strode toward them. Her brown eyes totally glowed. Darcy was always upbeat, but Stephanie had never seen her *this* happy before.

"He's so totally awesome!" Darcy exclaimed. "He's sweet and funny and nice—and totally gorgeous."

"I guess you like him a little," Stephanie teased.

"Oh, really? How could you tell?" Maura added.

Darcy ignored them. "I still can't believe he likes me."

"Why shouldn't he?" Stephanie demanded. "You're our best friend, aren't you?"

"A best friend with a birthday coming up," Allie added.

"Right. And we need to make plans," Stephanie said. "Let's see. Your birthday is two weeks from Tuesday. How about we take you out for pizza Tuesday night? Maybe to Tony's, or someplace casual."

4

Darcy looked uncomfortable. "I'm not sure, Steph." She hesitated. "It's really nice of you and all, but . . ."

"But what?" Allie prodded.

"But I was hoping Alex would take me out for my birthday," Darcy finished.

"Like to a fancy restaurant or something?" Maura asked.

"Oh, it could be anything," Darcy told her. "Just something that shows I'm special to him. As special as he is to me."

"Has he mentioned it yet?" Stephanie asked.

"No," Darcy answered. "But I told him when my birthday is. So, would you guys be mad if I left the night open? I really want to be with him." She flashed an enormous smile. "I just know this will be the best birthday of my entire life!"

"How could we mind that? It's your day," Stephanie said.

"Right," Allie agreed. "But we will get to do *something* together, won't we?"

"Sure," Darcy answered. "Let's plan next week, after the big track meet. I'm having a hard time thinking about anything else right now. Besides, I'm exhausted."

"How come?" Stephanie asked.

"Well, you know I've been running with Alex

early in the morning," Darcy replied. "To help him be in top shape for the meet. I love spending the time with him, but it's harder than I thought." She yawned widely.

"You mean, you're too tired to think about birthday plans?" Maura looked at her as if she were crazy.

"Yeah, believe it or not." Darcy grinned and glanced at her watch. "Wow. I'd better get going. I have a ton of homework, and I want to get home and take a nap before I dig in."

"We should all get going," Stephanie agreed. "Call me later, you guys!"

The phone rang the instant Stephanie walked into her kitchen. She grabbed the receiver and heard Allie's voice on the other end.

"Steph, I just had a horrible thought," Allie blurted out before Stephanie said a word. "What if Alex *doesn't* come up with a fabulous date for Darcy's birthday?"

"Why wouldn't he?" Stephanie asked. "I mean, he definitely seems to like Darcy."

"True," Allie said. "But guys can be dense about stuff like that. And Darcy has her heart set on something fabulous. She's so excited about it.

What if Alex totally forgets? Or what if he just plans some ordinary date? She'll be crushed! Her birthday will be totally ruined."

Stephanie slipped off her backpack and pulled over a kitchen chair. "You're right," she said as she sat down. "Do you think we should ask Alex if he has something planned?"

"I'd feel weird doing that," Allie told her.

"Me, too," Stephanie admitted. They were both silent for a minute. "I've got it!" Stephanie exclaimed.

"Got what?" Allie asked.

"*We'll* plan Darcy's birthday!" Stephanie felt a burst of excitement. "We'll throw her a huge surprise party! And we'll make Alex a part of it. We'll do most of the planning, but he can help us. Then Darcy will definitely feel like he did this great thing for her."

"And we'll be sure she's not disappointed," Allie added. "Steph, you're totally brilliant!"

"Thank you. It's a gift, isn't it?" Stephanie laughed. "Anyway, now we don't have to worry about a thing."

"Yeah. Except . . ." Allie's voice trailed off.

"Except what?" Stephanie asked.

"Well, what if Alex *is* the kind of guy who

wouldn't do something nice for Darcy's birthday," Allie suggested. "Shouldn't Allie find that out for herself?"

Stephanie laughed. "Allie, why are you so worried about something that hasn't even happened?"

"I don't know," Allie admitted. Her tone brightened. "You're right. It's dumb to worry. So let's do it! Let's throw Darcy the best party she's ever had!"

"All right!" Stephanie cheered. "I'll call Maura right away and tell her."

"Smile, Stephanie!"

Stephanie glanced up in surprise. Her nine-year-old sister, Michelle, danced around her. Michelle aimed a camera at Stephanie's face.

Flash!

Stephanie blinked. Bright lights danced across her eyes.

She quickly told Allie good-bye and turned to her sister. "Michelle, *what* are you doing?"

Michelle darted in the other direction, snapping another picture. Her strawberry-blond ponytail bobbed as she stooped down for a low shot.

"I'm taking your picture from different angles," Michelle replied. "A photographer has to frame a bunch of shots to see which comes out best."

"Since when are you a photographer?" Stephanie asked. She got up to get herself a soda and some chips.

"Since today," Michelle replied. She framed Stephanie in another shot. "Our art teacher is teaching us about photography. And guess what?"

"What?" Stephanie asked. She really wanted to start planning the most fabulous party in the world. But Michelle was really excited. She knew Michelle wouldn't stop bugging her unless she paid attention.

Michelle grinned. "Our photo project is called *A Week in the Life of . . .*"

"The life of who?" Stephanie asked.

"You!" Michelle exclaimed. "It's a big honor."

"Wait a minute," Stephanie said. "What do I have to do for this big honor?"

"Nothing," Michelle told her. "I'm supposed to take pictures of you just being yourself."

"For a whole week? I don't know," Stephanie began. Michelle snapped another picture.

"Do you have to start right now?" Stephanie asked.

"Yup," Michelle replied. "Just pretend I'm not here." She snapped another shot.

"That's going to be a little hard," Stephanie said. The phone rang again. Stephanie grabbed it.

Snap! Snap!

"I have a feeling I'll be taking a lot of *phone* shots," Michelle muttered.

Stephanie ignored her. "Hello?" she spoke into the receiver.

"Steph, it's me, Darcy. You've got to help me! You have to run with Alex tomorrow morning!"

"*Me*, run with Alex!" Stephanie exclaimed. "Why?"

Snap!

Stephanie frowned. She waved Michelle away.

"My mother caught me taking a nap," Darcy reported. "And she got all bent out of shape. She says these early mornings are too much for me. She wants me to stop running with him."

"Maybe you should," Stephanie said. "If you're that tired."

"I can't!" Darcy wailed. "I was the one who convinced him to put in the extra practice. If I wimp out, he'll think I'm a total jerk."

"Why can't he go by himself?" Stephanie asked.

"Well, this will sound dumb." Darcy paused. "But Alex *hates* getting up early. He didn't want to do it at all. But this is the first chance we've ever had to win the regionals. I really want to make sure we win."

"I don't see how I can help," Stephanie said. "I

hate getting up early, too. And I don't run nearly as fast as you."

"That doesn't matter," Darcy said. "Please, Steph, don't let me down. I talked my mom into letting me go two days a week. But you have to do the other three for me," Darcy pleaded. "If you go, I can at least tell Alex I found a substitute."

"I guess it means a lot to you," Stephanie said. "Oh, all right. What time do we go?"

"Six in the morning," Darcy said.

"Six!" Stephanie shrieked. It was hard enough to get up for school at seven. Six was outrageous.

Michelle snapped another picture. "Wow! You should've seen the expression on your face," she said.

Stephanie turned her back to Michelle. "Okay, six," she reluctantly agreed.

"Well, you'll have to wake up *before* six if you want to start running *at* six," Darcy pointed out. "But I'll tell Alex to meet you on the corner of Wells and Horton, right near your house. That should give you a bit more time."

"Thanks," Stephanie muttered. "The things I do for my friends." She hung up, shaking her head. How would she ever get up so early? Oh, well, it was for a good cause. And there wasn't anything she wouldn't do for Darcy. After all, they were best friends.

CHAPTER

2

◆ ◀ ✦ ◆

"Earth to Stephanie! Come in!"

The sound of D.J.'s voice jolted Stephanie back to reality. Her older sister stood in front of her, waving a hand in front of Stephanie's eyes. "Welcome back," she said with a smile. "What were you thinking about so seriously?"

It was long after supper. Stephanie sat at the kitchen table, trying to work on her party list.

"I'm trying to plan a surprise party for Darcy," Stephanie explained.

"That sounds great," D.J. said. "Maybe I'll come—and show off my new hair."

Stephanie peered at her more closely. "Wow,

Deej! You put a streak in your hair," she said.

There was a definite blond streak in the front of D.J.'s short, light brown hair.

"Do you like it?" D.J. asked.

"Yeah," Stephanie told her. "Definitely cool enough for Darcy's party." She knew D.J. wasn't serious about going. After all, her sister was a college student. She didn't exactly party with middle-school kids.

"So, tell me all the party plans," D.J. urged.

Before Stephanie could answer, the kitchen door swung open. Her uncle Jesse came in. "Did I hear party?" he asked. "Man, when I was in high school, we had the best parties."

Stephanie didn't doubt it. Jesse was married to her aunt Becky, and they had twin boys—her cousins Nicky and Alex. But sometimes he didn't seem at all like a grown-up. He was more like a big kid. He loved to party!

Jesse was her mother's brother. He came to help take care of Stephanie and her sisters after their mother died. She was glad he and her aunt stayed in the attic apartment even after the twins were born.

Jesse pulled open the refrigerator door. "I remember one party where the address was misprinted on the invitations. The entire junior class descended on this poor older couple down the block."

"Oh, no!" D.J. said, chuckling. "What did they do?"

Jesse laughed. "They got into it and wound up having the party at their house!" D.J. and Stephanie laughed, too. Stephanie could just picture these old people whooping it up with a bunch of high school kids.

"Hey, what's all the laughing about?" Joey Gladstone asked as he came in the back door from the yard. "I'm not even telling one of my fantastic jokes!"

Joey was a comedian. He'd been joking around ever since Stephanie could remember. Joey was Stephanie's dad's best friend in college. He'd also moved in to help raise the girls.

"I was telling them that story about the party that ended up at the Carters' house," Jesse filled him in.

"I know that story," Joey said. He bent forward and spoke as though he had no teeth. "Come on, kids! Get down and boogie!" He danced around the kitchen as if he were ninety years old.

"Don't worry." Stephanie giggled. "I'll make sure everyone knows our address for *this* party."

"Excuse me?" Danny Tanner appeared in the

doorway. "Exactly what party is happening here?"

"Dad!" Stephanie stopped laughing. "I was going to ask you tonight. Do you think I could give Darcy a surprise party here?"

Danny's brow wrinkled. "Here?" he asked.

"Uh-oh," Joey warned. "Watch out, Stephanie. You're talking to the only guy who ever arrived at a college party carrying a handheld vacuum cleaner."

"Well, just that once," Danny shot back. "But that dorm room was a real pigsty!"

Stephanie hid her smile. Her father was a total neat freak. He hated messes. She could picture him moving through a wild party, dusting and tidying as he went.

"What kind of party will this be?" Danny asked Stephanie.

"I'm not sure yet," she answered. "I just started thinking about it. I don't have a theme or anything. I—"

"No problem," D.J. interrupted. "I have a stack of my old *Teen Blast* magazines in my closet. There's a party suggestion in every issue. Come on, I'll give them to you."

Stephanie followed D.J. out the kitchen door. "Don't worry about Dad," D.J. whispered as they crossed the living room. "Remember, he always says no at first. Just stay calm. Give him a list of exactly how many kids are coming and exactly what you plan to do. Then he'll give in and say yes."

"Thanks, Deej. I forgot," Stephanie said. Sometimes it was great having an older sister who knew how to manage certain things—like their father.

"Smile!" Michelle popped up from behind the couch and snapped a picture.

Stephanie was so startled, she bumped into D.J. "Michelle!" she scolded. "Can't you give me some warning?"

"Nope," Michelle answered. "This is a candid photo essay. The idea is to capture the moment. Take a shot when you're *not* expecting it."

"I'm going to capture *you* and put you in the closet if you scare me like that again," Stephanie warned.

She continued up the stairs behind D.J. "You should be flattered that Michelle picked you for her project," D.J. said as they headed for her room.

"I am, but she keeps popping up all over the place," Stephanie said. "It's getting annoying."

D.J. bent into her bedroom closet and scooped up a four-inch stack of magazines. She handed them to Stephanie. "I'm sure you'll find some good ideas in here."

Stephanie thanked her and carried the magazines to the room she shared with Michelle. She dropped them onto her bed and began leafing through the party sections.

"'Cool Hula Party,'" she read. Pretty corny. She tossed that issue aside and opened the next one. "'Rock Video Madness,'" she read. That had possibilities.

Michelle wandered in and snapped a picture. "I'll call this one 'Stephanie Deep in Thought,'" Michelle announced, suggesting a title for the picture. "Or I could call it `Party Planning Madness.'"

"Try calling it `Party Planning Confusion,'" Stephanie replied. "There are so many good ideas here, I can't decide which to choose."

Michelle put her camera aside and began changing into her nightshirt. "Can I be the photographer at the party?" she asked.

"No way!" Stephanie shook her head. "My friends don't want a little kid bothering them all night."

"Oh, excuse me." Michelle climbed into bed. "I forgot I wasn't cool enough."

"Would you want Nicky and Alex at *your* party?" Stephanie countered.

17

"They aren't old enough to take pictures," Michelle argued. Stephanie sighed. "Good night, Michelle."

"Night," Michelle mumbled.

Stephanie opened another issue of *Teen Blast*.

Picking a theme for this party is a lot harder than I thought it would be, she thought. And she had a dozen more magazines to go!

What is that awful sound? Stephanie rolled over in bed and knocked some magazines onto the floor.

She blinked and yawned. Oh—that awful sound was her alarm clock blaring in her ear.

But it's still dark out! she thought. *What's going on?*

She batted the clock a few times and finally hit the Off button.

"What's happening?" Michelle asked, rolling sleepily toward Stephanie.

"The alarm went off," Stephanie explained in a croaky morning voice. "Go back to sleep."

With a yawn Michelle rolled over again.

Sitting up in bed, Stephanie slowly remembered. She set the alarm for five-thirty. She was supposed to meet Alex for their morning run.

Oh, why did I ever agree to this? she wondered.

Miserably, she forced her sleepy body to move out of bed.

Her eyes were half closed as she dressed in gray sweat pants, a stained blue sweatshirt, and battered sneakers. Groggily, she glanced at her face in the mirror on her closet door. Her hair was a mess. Her eyes were totally puffed up.

Who cares? she thought, trudging out the door. *It's too early to care.*

By the time she stepped outside, the first gold and pink slashes of dawn light were streaking across the gray sky. The cool air wakened her as she headed to the corner to meet Alex. Still, her feet dragged.

She was almost half a block away, when she spotted him already waiting. Despite the morning chill, he wore shorts and a T-shirt.

She suddenly felt awkward and shy. *This is kind of weird*, she thought as she hurried toward him. *We really don't know each other.*

"Hi!" Alex called as she neared him. "You're Stephanie, right?"

"Right," she replied.

"Darcy said you'd be on time." Alex grinned. He looked adorable, Stephanie noted. And a lot more awake than she felt.

She forced herself to grin back.

"Anyway, I made sure I got here a bit early," Alex went on. "I didn't want you to wait here alone."

"Thanks. You didn't have to do that," Stephanie told him. *That was really thoughtful,* she told herself.

"And you didn't have to do this," Alex replied. "I appreciate it and all, but Darcy is the one set on this morning run. Not me. I wouldn't blame you if you turned around and went back home. You could get another hour of sleep."

"I'm pretty much awake now," she said, realizing it was true. "I don't think I could sleep again."

"Me neither," he agreed. "Getting up is torture. But once I'm up, I almost enjoy it."

Stephanie laughed. Alex was making her feel a lot more cheerful.

"Guess we might as well run," he added.

"Might as well," Stephanie agreed. "But don't feel like you have to wait for me to catch up."

"I won't," Alex said. "I practice for speed when I get to school. This run is to build up my endurance. That's my weakness in track."

"Really?" she said.

"Yup."

Side by side, they began jogging through the

hilly San Francisco streets. Alex explained the difference between training for long-distance running and sprinting.

The streets were mostly empty. They passed an occasional person walking a dog. Or shop owners unlocking their stores. Stephanie realized Alex was keeping an easy pace for her sake. But she had to work to keep up with him.

"Are you okay?" he asked as they climbed a steep hill.

"Doing fine," she replied breathlessly. "How . . . can . . . you talk . . ."

"And run at the same time?" Alex finished for her. He grinned. "I've been in training all year, remember?"

Stephanie nodded. They didn't talk much for a while. She had the feeling Alex was being kind. He obviously knew she couldn't keep up *and* talk.

"I like this time of morning," he finally said. "I never knew that before Darcy started this run. I should thank her. It's nice being up before everyone else."

A half hour earlier, Stephanie would never have agreed with him. But it *was* nice to watch the sun rise higher in the sky. And she loved the quiet.

Still, she was glad as they finally headed back home.

"You know, I almost feel like we're friends already," Alex commented. "Darcy talks about you all the time."

"Darcy's great," Stephanie said.

"Yeah," he agreed. "And you're a great runner," he added.

"No way," she said, grinning.

Alex shook his head. "Seriously, you're easy to keep pace with. Some runners speed up, then slow down. But you keep a nice, steady pace. That makes this more fun."

"Really?" Stephanie felt pleased at the compliment. "I guess it *was* fun," she said in surprise.

The corner where they had to split up came into view.

Why not ask about the party now? she suddenly thought. "Alex," she blurted out as they jogged. "How would you like to help me and my friends throw Darcy a surprise birthday party?"

"Wow!" Alex stopped jogging completely. "I completely forgot about her birthday!"

"We decided to have it the Saturday after the meet," Stephanie reminded him.

"You can definitely count me in," Alex told her. "And thanks."

He did forget, Stephanie thought. *But I'm glad I reminded him in time.*

"Listen," Alex told her. "You don't really have to do this run again."

"It's okay, I liked it," Stephanie said. She was actually sorry their run was done.

"I had a good time, too." Alex grinned. His unusual eyes sparkled as he gazed at her.

Wow. His eyes are *incredible,* she thought.

"Well, I can deal with getting up at dawn—if you promise to win the meet on Saturday," she told him.

"Deal!" Alex laughed. With a wave, he jogged away from her, disappearing around the corner.

She stared after him, grinning. He really *was* sweet! No wonder Darcy was so crazy about him.

CHAPTER

3

◆ ◥ ◆ ◆

"It's really strange, but I think I have more energy than usual." Stephanie slammed her locker and turned toward Darcy. They had only a few minutes before the first morning bell sounded.

Darcy shifted the books in her arms. "It works that way sometimes," she agreed. "At first I was energized, too. But you might get tired by late afternoon."

They began walking toward Stephanie's homeroom. "Anyway, thanks for filling in for me," Darcy added.

"No problem. It was fun," Stephanie assured her. "Alex was great. Now I can see why you like him."

Darcy's eyes lit up with pleasure. "Really? I'm glad. I want my friends to like each other."

Briiiing!

The bell sounded and Darcy waved good-bye. Stephanie didn't see her again until lunchtime. By then, she was dying to talk about the party with Allie and Maura. She finally got a chance when Darcy went off to talk to Alex.

Alex was sitting with the guys from the track team. Stephanie glanced at his table. Their eyes met and he waved. With a quick smile, she waved back.

"Well?" Maura demanded. "How was the run?" She and Allie leaned forward.

"Great," Stephanie reported. "And it's a good thing I asked Alex to help with the party. He totally forgot Darcy's birthday was coming."

"See?" Allie said. "I told you he would. Darcy should date Ben. He wouldn't forget an important thing like a birthday."

"How do you know that?" Maura asked.

"Well, I can't believe Spencer would forget *my* birthday," Allie replied. "And Ben is his best friend. So they're probably alike."

"Allie, that makes no sense at all." Stephanie grinned. "Alex is a good guy, even if he did forget.

So now we have to get the party plans rolling."

"Did your dad give you permission yet?" Allie asked.

"This morning, after I came back from my run," Stephanie replied. "I had to promise things wouldn't get too wild, though. Can you guys come over this afternoon? We'll have our first party-planning session."

Maura and Allie agreed quickly. Darcy was headed back to their table.

"He's just the best," she said with a dreamy sigh. "I never get tired of talking to him. And he calls me practically every night, too!" She slid into her seat and finished the last of her juice box.

"Don't look now, Allie, but here comes Spencer," Maura said. "And Ben."

Allie looked up eagerly as Spencer came closer. His auburn hair was almost the same color as hers. He pushed back his glasses and flashed a friendly smile, Stephanie noted. His friend Ben was thin and much taller, with dark hair.

"Hi, Spencer. Hi, Ben," Stephanie greeted them. Spencer slid into the empty chair beside Allie and took her hand.

Stephanie smiled to herself. They made a really cute couple. She was glad they were seeing each other.

"Hi, Stephanie." Ben stood awkwardly by the table. He cleared his throat. "Hi, Darcy."

Darcy smiled politely, then went back to her lunch.

"Allie, do you still want to study for that history test together?" Spencer asked.

"Sure, come to my house after supper," Allie agreed. "You can come, too, Ben."

"Oh, that's okay," Ben replied, looking embarrassed. "I don't want to get in the way."

Allie tossed her napkin at him. "We're just studying."

"What if Darcy comes?" Allie asked. She turned to Darcy. "Can you make it, Darce?" she asked.

"Uh . . . no," Darcy replied. "I can't."

"Actually, I can't either," Ben told Allie. "I study better by myself."

"Okay, but come if you change your mind," Allie told him. Ben nodded. Then he and Spencer left to get to their next class. Allie turned toward Darcy. "Ben really is sweet," she said.

Stephanie groaned. "Al, give it a break. Darcy happens to be crazy about someone else."

"Too bad." Allie sighed. "Ben is so nice!"

"Alex is nicer," Darcy insisted. Everyone laughed.

* * *

"Look through these first," Stephanie suggested. She handed Maura and Allie six issues of *Teen Blast* magazine. "I picked out the ones with the best party suggestions. Why don't you see which ones you like?"

She popped open a soda as they thumbed through the magazines.

Maura sat forward. "This dessert party sounds so romantic," she said. She held out the Valentine's Day issue.

"Yeah, but this is a party, not a romantic dinner for two," Allie pointed out.

"You can have a romantic party," Maura insisted. "Everyone comes dressed up. We play soft music and serve sophisticated, delicious desserts—and act like human beings for a change."

"That *would* be a switch." Allie giggled.

"I don't know. Do you think our friends could handle something so . . . so . . . civilized?" Stephanie asked doubtfully.

"It's about time they learned," Maura replied.

Stephanie opened a summer issue and handed it to Maura. "Check out this Mexican Chili Fiesta. I think it looks like the most fun of all."

As Maura read, her nose wrinkled. "I don't think so. It just doesn't seem very Darcy-ish to me."

"Really?" Stephanie shook her head. "I think it's more Darcy-like than the dessert party. That could put everyone to sleep!"

"It would be cool and grown-up," Maura argued.

Stephanie looked to Allie. "What do you think?"

Allie considered. "Why not have chili first and then serve romantic desserts?"

"What a great idea!" Stephanie exclaimed.

"It's settled, then," Maura declared. "But should the party be a surprise, or are we telling Darcy?"

"Surprise," Stephanie and Allie replied together.

"Great. And are we actually involving Alex in this, or is that just a story we're telling Darcy?" Maura asked.

"We have to involve him," Allie said. "Why should he get the praise if he does none of the work?"

"He said he's happy to help," Stephanie reminded them. "I'll talk to him about the details on Thursday. That's when we run together again."

"Okay. I suppose our next step is to buy invitations and decorations," Allie went on. "Want to go to the party store Thursday after school?"

"Sure," Stephanie agreed.

"This will be so awesome!" Maura gathered her things together. She and Allie headed for the front door.

"I think so, too," Stephanie agreed, walking across the room with them. "See you tomorrow!"

She closed the door and leaned against it. Her mind was racing with party plans. *We'll have to make a list of food to buy next*, she was thinking as the front door bell rang.

Somebody forgot something, she thought, flinging the door open.

Alex!

"Hey," she greeted him in surprise.

"Hey, yourself," Alex replied. He plucked a paper from his back pocket. "We got the schedule of events for the track meet today. I was on my way home from practice and thought maybe you'd like to see it."

"Sure." She took the paper from him. "Thanks. Listen, I wanted to talk to you about Darcy's party. Do you have a minute?"

Alex nodded and stepped into the living room. Stephanie showed him to the couch and offered him a soda.

"Did you see Allie and Maura?" she asked. "They just left. We had the *best* party idea!"

"Oh, yeah? Alex flipped open a soda. He glanced at the neat stack of CDs on the corner of the coffee table. "Hey, do you like *Vanishing Moon*, too?" he asked.

"Like them? I love them," Stephanie replied. "I saw their new video on TV last week and rushed out to buy this CD."

"I didn't even know it was out yet," Alex said. "Oh, man! I've got to get this."

Stephanie shook her head in disbelief. "No one else I know even *likes* them."

"They're fantastic," Alex declared. "Elliot Moon's voice is totally amazing."

"Totally," Stephanie agreed. It was great to have another fan to discuss her favorite group with!

"Not only his voice is unbelievable," Alex went on. "What really slays me are his lyrics. Catch this one . . ." He began to read from the lyric notes in the CD case.

"That's my favorite song!" Stephanie exclaimed in excitement. It was a very poetic love song. In the lyrics, the man saw his beloved's face in the stars and kissed the water that reflected them.

I can't believe a guy like Alex would admit he likes those lyrics, she thought. *He really is amazing.*

Alex finished reading the lyrics. "Awesome, huh?"

"It's beautiful," Stephanie said.

Alex listed the other CDs he owned—including early ones Stephanie had never heard of. "My brother was into them when they first came out," he explained. "He got me into them, too."

Stephanie glanced at her watch. They'd been talking for over a half hour! That was fine with her. She could talk about *Vanishing Moon* forever.

"You have to hear their first CD," Alex urged her. "You can't get it anymore, but my brother has it."

"Wow. I'd *love* to!" Stephanie exclaimed.

Snap!

"Say cheese!" Michelle popped up from behind the couch and took a picture of Stephanie and Alex.

Stephanie laughed at Alex's shocked expression. "It's for her school project," she explained. "She's documenting a week in my life. Sorry if she scared you, Alex."

"Oh, *you're* Alex," Michelle said. "Then I should title this picture 'Stephanie with Her Best Friend's Boyfriend.'"

"Don't say that," Alex said with a chuckle. "That might not sound too good."

Michelle frowned. "No? Why not?"

"You know. It might give someone the wrong idea," Alex said.

"Why don't you call it 'Stephanie and Alex Talking About Music,'" Stephanie suggested.

"If you even use that picture," Alex said.

"Why wouldn't I?" Michelle asked.

Alex shrugged and stood up. "I can't believe I've been here so long. Sorry for blabbing so much," he told Stephanie.

"No problem," Stephanie said. "I've never found another *Vanishing Moon* fan to talk to before."

He nodded. "I'm definitely lending you the early CDs. You'll go crazy over them."

Stephanie walked with him to the door. "See you Thursday for our run," he said.

"Thursday," she replied.

He hesitated, then put his hand on her arm. "Michelle won't show that picture around, will she?"

"No, it's just for her class," she replied.

"Okay. Good," he said, then smiled and left.

Stephanie closed the door. *Why was he so worried about that photo?* she wondered. *Oh, well. It was no big deal.*

CHAPTER
4

◆ ◀ ★ ◆

Snap!

"Mich-elle!" Stephanie complained. "Would you knock it off!" She struggled as their dog, Comet, tried to yank himself out of her hands. They were out in the backyard.

Comet had run through some mud during their walk together. Stephanie was trying to spray him off with the garden hose. But the more she tried to get him to stand still, the more he jumped around, spraying mud all over her.

"This is great action," Michelle muttered. *Snap!* She took another picture.

"Stop it! I mean it, Michelle," Stephanie insisted. "I'm a total mess! I don't want my picture

34

taken!" As she spoke, Comet bumped his nose into the hose and sent a stream of water shooting into her face. "Arrgghh!" she groaned.

"Taking care of Comet is part of your week," Michelle countered. "This is a true-to-life record of your real life."

Danny stepped into the yard. "Dad," Stephanie began, "would you tell Michelle not to —"

"Steph, you have a visitor," Danny cut her off.

Alex stepped into view. He smiled at the sight of Stephanie's tangled, muddy hair and spattered clothes.

"Hey, sorry." He grinned. "Looks like you're in the middle of puppy-bath time. I brought you those CDs we talked about." He set a white plastic bag on the picnic table. He glanced at Comet, who was still scampering around Stephanie. "What's this cute guy's name?"

"Comet," Michelle told him.

"Come here, Comet," Alex called. Comet jumped up, planting his wet, muddy paws on Alex's pants.

"Comet, no!" Stephanie scolded.

Alex laughed. "That's okay. I have a dog, too. I know how it is." He took the hose from Stephanie and stuck his thumb in the spout. The water sprayed in a fine mist. Comet danced happily beneath it. In a few minutes, he was clean.

"Excellent!" Stephanie proclaimed, wiping mud from her cheek. "That was clever of you."

"I do this to my dog all the time." Alex set the hose down. He sat on the bench by the picnic table. "I missed you this morning," he told her. "Somehow, I don't run as smoothly with Darcy. It's like she and I keep tripping each other."

"That's odd," Stephanie said, not quite knowing how to reply. She turned off the faucet by the house. "Darcy's a much better athlete than I am."

"I guess," Alex said.

"Since you're here, we should go over the party guest list," Stephanie suggested. "Maura, Allie, and I wrote it up at lunchtime while Darcy was talking to you." She happened to have it folded in her back jeans pocket. Shaking water from her hands, she gingerly lifted it out and handed it to him. "You might want to add some names to it," she offered as he read it through.

He looked up from the list and frowned. "This Spencer kid—does he wear glasses?" he asked. Stephanie nodded. "And he hangs with a geek named Ben?"

"Ben's his best friend," she confirmed. "Do you think he's a geek?"

"Definitely," Alex said. "Do we have to invite them?"

"Yeah, sort of," she answered. "Spencer is Allie's new boyfriend. And Ben kind of goes along with him."

"They are such major geekoids," Alex complained. "There are a couple of other loser types on this list, too."

"Losers?" Stephanie couldn't imagine who he meant. She liked everyone on the list.

Alex took a short pencil from his jeans pocket. "I'll put a question mark next to some of these names. Then you can decide what you want to do. I'll also add some guys from the track team—and some girls I know from the cheerleading squad."

"Okay," Stephanie agreed. She wasn't sure how she felt about him calling her friends geeks. On the other hand, he was entitled to his opinion. She sat beside him on the bench, looking to see whose names he added and whose received a question mark.

"Say cheese, you guys!" Michelle snapped a photo of the two of them turning toward her with startled expressions.

"Hey, catch me," Alex clowned. "I'm a male magazine model!"

He started hamming for the camera.

Stephanie grinned as he struck one comic pose after the other. He pretended to catch an invisible football. He tossed his head back and shouted with phony laughter. He sucked his cheeks in and half shut his eyes, imitating a movie star.

Michelle snapped away.

Wow, Stephanie thought. *He's totally gorgeous, a great athlete, he likes Vanishing Moon, he's good with pets, and he's funny, too.* His good points kept adding up. Amazing.

"What's going on?" Becky appeared in the yard, a giant smile on her face. Alex's face turned red in embarrassment. He dropped the movie star pose.

"Aunt Becky, this is Alex," Stephanie introduced them.

"Hi. Hey, I know you," Alex said. "You're on *Wake Up, San Francisco*, aren't you?"

"Yes, that's me," Aunt Becky said. She and Danny were co-hosts on the morning TV chat and news show.

"I watch you every morning," Alex went on. "My whole family does. You and that guy, Danny, are great."

"That guy Danny is my dad," Michelle told him.

"No! That's totally awesome!" Alex cried. "I can't believe I'm in the home of TV stars."

Becky smiled. "Stars! Hey, I like your new boyfriend, Stephanie."

"Oh, no," Stephanie said quickly. "He's not my boy—"

Aunt Becky didn't hear. She was listening to Alex recall his favorite episodes of the TV show. "Alex, why don't you stay for dinner tonight?" Becky suggested. "We can talk more about the show—if you're really interested."

Stephanie waved her arms to stop her aunt. "He wouldn't want to —"

"Cool!" Alex said. "There's tons of stuff I want to ask about the show."

"Great." Becky turned to Stephanie. "He's cute," she whispered.

Stephanie felt her cheeks flush in embarrassment.

"You never told me you were related to famous TV stars," Alex commented when Becky went back inside.

"I don't think of them as famous," she explained. "Are you sure you want to stay for supper?"

"Absolutely. Hey, want to listen to those CDs?" he suggested.

"Yeah—as soon as I put on some dry clothes," she replied. "Meanwhile, check out this chili recipe I found. You can tell me what you think after I change."

"Then it's definitely a Mexican chili party?" he asked.

"Yup," she said as they went inside together. "Dancing, Mexican chili, and then romantic desserts."

"Sounds perfect," Alex declared.

My entire family thinks Alex is great, Stephanie thought as she gazed across the dinner table.

Danny and Becky loved talking to him about their show. Joey loved telling all the jokes the family had heard dozens of times—and Alex loved hearing them all. He thought they were hilarious! And he was totally impressed that Jesse once had a rock band. Jesse promised to play for him after dinner.

Michelle and D.J. liked him. And so did the twins! Little Alex loved that they had the same name. And Nicky wouldn't leave him alone for a second.

After dinner, it was Stephanie's turn to clear. "I'll help you," Alex offered.

"Now, that's a great guy," D.J. commented as she left the table.

"Hand me the dishes and I'll rinse them for the dishwasher," Stephanie suggested.

They worked in comfortable silence for a few minutes. "You know," Alex began, "I'm a little nervous about the track meet."

"How come?" Stephanie asked. "You're in great shape."

"It's just that everyone is expecting me to win this thing," he said. "I mean, it's a lot of pressure."

"Yes, but I bet you will," she encouraged. "Not that I want to add more pressure," she quickly added.

Alex shook his head. "No, you're helping. The other day when we ran, I felt completely relaxed for the first time in a long time."

"Really?" Stephanie turned away from him and rinsed an already clean plate in the sink. Sometimes he said things—nice things—that made her feel ill at ease.

I don't know if he should say those things to me, she thought. *After all, he is Darcy's boyfriend. It's almost like he's flirting with me.*

Stephanie reached over and slid the plate into the top rack of the dishwasher. Alex placed his hand on top of hers, holding it in place.

Oh, my goodness, she thought. A jolt of excitement, like electricity, shot through her. She glanced up at him, but he didn't seem to notice a thing. In fact, she wasn't sure he even realized his hand was on top of hers.

"Now we just have to wipe up, and we're done," was all he said.

Stephanie stared at him. He had to feel her hand beneath his. Didn't he?

Slowly, she slid her hand away and took a sponge from the sink ledge. "I'll stack, you wipe," she said, working to keep her voice steady. She handed him the sponge.

He nodded and went over to wipe off the table. She sneaked a few looks at him, then glanced down at her hand. It was as if she could still feel the warmth of his hand where it had covered hers.

Why did he do that? she wondered in confusion.

He was supposed to like Darcy. He was Darcy's boyfriend.

But that wasn't the most confusing part. What really upset her was the way her stomach flipped over at his touch.

What's the matter with you? she scolded herself. *You and Alex are just friends! He's Darcy's guy.*

Friends, she thought. *That's all we'll ever be.*

CHAPTER
5

◆ ◀ ◆ ◆

". . . seven, eight, nine, ten," Stephanie counted as she brushed her hair with strong, quick strokes. She flipped her head back and wrapped it in a scrunchie.

Ugh, that looks dumb, she decided, gazing in the mirror. She yanked out the scrunchie and let her hair fall softly around her face. *Much better,* she thought.

She pulled on pale yellow nylon shorts and a purple tank top. A little mascara, some lip gloss, and she was ready to go.

Snap! Flash!

"Not again!" She whirled to face Michelle.

"What are you doing up so early?" she demanded.

Michelle scratched her side through her night-shirt. "I have to photograph your *whole* day," Michelle reminded her. "I think I'll call this one 'The Runner Prepares.'"

"That flash just about blinded me!" Stephanie complained. She rubbed her eyes, careful not to smear her mascara.

"Sorry," Michelle said. "Are you running with Alex again?"

"Yes, and I'll be late if I don't get out of here," Stephanie said, heading for the door

"Wait up!" Michelle pulled on some jeans and stuffed her nightshirt into them. "I'm coming with you."

"No way!" Stephanie objected.

"But running with Alex is part of your week," Michelle insisted. She shoved her feet into sneakers without bothering with socks. "I can't leave it out of my project."

Stephanie groaned. "You won't be able to keep up with us," she warned.

"I'll ride my bike," Michelle said.

"Come on, Michelle," Stephanie pleaded. "Give me a break, please? Don't come."

"You won't even know I'm there," Michelle told her.

Stephanie sighed. Once Michelle set her mind to something, it was nearly impossible to change it. "I'm not waiting for you," she declared. "So come at your own risk."

"No problem." Michelle slung the camera strap around her neck. "Ready!"

Stephanie hurried down the steps and rushed outside. Michelle wasn't behind her. *Great*, she thought. *She gave up!*

A second later, Michelle appeared around the side of the house, riding her bike.

This is so embarrassing, Stephanie grumbled to herself.

She headed down the street, lost in thought. She remembered how Alex branded some of the kids on the party list geeks. It made her uncomfortable. Part of her knew that she shouldn't care what somebody else thought. In fact, it was pretty rude to call someone's friends geeks.

But mostly, she *did* care what Alex thought. What if he thought she was a geek, too? A geek who couldn't lose her tag-along little sister?

She caught sight of Alex waiting before she reached the corner. He smiled and waved.

She caught her breath. Seeing him sent a rush of happiness through her.

Stop it, she scolded herself. *What are you getting so*

worked up about? It's only Alex—Darcy's boyfriend. Alex is just a friend, nothing to get all excited about.

But it's all right to feel happy to see a friend, she argued with herself. *There's nothing wrong with that. I'm always glad to see Allie, Maura, and Darcy.*

Yeah, but not this *happy,* a voice inside her insisted.

This more than just being glad to see a friend.

I will not feel anything special, she ordered herself. *I don't like this feeling. I want it to go away!*

She joined Alex. His smile faded when he caught sight of Michelle.

"I don't mind Michelle coming along," he said. "She's a cool kid. But that camera has got to go."

She turned to Michelle. "Michelle, could you please—" she began.

Snap!

Michelle took a picture of Alex and Stephanie standing together.

Alex shook his head. "Listen," he quietly told Stephanie, "we'll just have to ditch her."

"You're on," she agreed. "Go!"

She put on a blast of speed and raced down the block. Alex was right by her side. Then slightly ahead of her. They careened around a corner, took a sharp right turn, and headed back the way they came.

Stephanie was moving so fast, she surprised herself. She glanced back. No sign of Michelle! She slowed to a stop and stood panting, catching her breath.

"Wow!" Alex laughed, slowing down alongside her. "What a sprinter! You should be on the team."

"Thanks," she gasped out. She leaned back against a tree.

"I think you're the most awesome girl I've ever met," he said. Their eyes met. She felt another electric current pass through her.

Watch out! a voice inside her screamed. *Don't flirt with him!*

She pushed away from the tree. "We'd better keep running," she said.

He nodded. They started jogging at a slower pace, just like the last time.

For the rest of the run, they barely spoke. Stephanie was worried. Was Alex annoyed? She had totally ignored his compliment.

She could have treated it like a friendly remark. She could have punched him in the arm playfully and said, "You're awesome, too."

Oh, it doesn't matter now, she told herself. She'd acted like a jerk and that was the end of it. If he didn't like her anymore, that was probably the best thing.

Then why did it feel so bad?

They reached the corner where they started from. Alex turned to head back toward his house.

He's not even going to say good-bye, Stephanie thought. She felt a wave of heaviness.

Then he turned toward her again.

"Listen, do you mind if I come by this afternoon?" he asked.

Yesss! she cheered inside. He wasn't mad at her!

"I don't mind," she answered. "Oh! But I won't be home," she added. "Allie, Maura, and I are going shopping for party decorations and invitations today."

"I'll join you guys, then," he volunteered. "I'm supposed to be helping with this thing, too. Right?"

"Well, y-yeah. Right," she stammered. "Okay, meet us at the party store around three-thirty."

"Cool. See you then." With a wave, he was off, jogging up the street.

Stephanie stood on the corner a moment, trying to make sense of her conflicting feelings.

You might as well be honest with yourself, she decided.

You have a whopping crush on Alex.

And she had the definite feeling he liked her, too.

But maybe not. It was possible that he hadn't even realized he'd placed his hand on hers the

other night. And he might have just compli-
mented her as a friend.

Maybe she was jumping to a totally wrong con-
clusion. Maybe she only thought *he* might like
her—because *she* liked *him*.

That's it, she assured herself. He liked her only
as a friend. And she would have to ignore her
crush.

She'd simply stop herself from feeling the way
she did. Each time she thought of him, she'd force
herself to think of Darcy instead.

That should do it, she told herself. *Thinking of
Darcy will destroy any romantic feelings I have for
Alex.*

She felt suddenly calmer. That afternoon would
be no problem. Allie and Maura would be there.
Having company would put the whole event on a
very friendly level.

Good. That's how it should be.

CHAPTER
6

◆ ◢ ✦ ◆

Stephanie bounded happily up her front steps.

Snap!

"The runner, home from her morning jog," Michelle announced behind her.

"Michelle! I forgot all about you," Stephanie admitted. "Are you mad that we ditched you?"

"Not really," Michelle said. "I knew you had to come back sometime. A good photojournalist is patient. She never gives up."

Stephanie shook her head. "Michelle, is every kid in your class taking this assignment so seriously?" she asked, sitting on the stoop. Michelle sat beside her.

"How should I know?" Michelle replied.

"Well, what I mean is—maybe you don't have to be with me every single moment," Stephanie suggested.

"I'm not with you all day at school," Michelle reminded her.

"I know. But could you not take pictures of me when I'm with Alex?" she asked. "He doesn't like to have his picture taken. He said so."

"He's lying," Michelle said. "He liked it yesterday in the yard. I never saw a bigger ham." She grinned.

Stephanie realized Michelle was right. Alex was happy to pose yesterday.

"Maybe he just doesn't like being in photos with you," Michelle suggested.

"That's crazy. Why wouldn't he want to be in pictures with me?" Stephanie asked.

"I don't know." Michelle shrugged. "Maybe he thinks you're funny-looking." With a grin, she ducked inside.

"Oh, ha-ha, Michelle! You're a riot," Stephanie called after her. She propped her chin on her hands. She hated to admit it, but Michelle had a point. Alex seemed annoyed with the picture-taking only when he and Stephanie were together.

Was he uncomfortable about his feelings for

her? As uncomfortable as she was about the way she felt for him?

Did he feel guilty, too?

Behind her, the door opened and D.J. appeared, heading to her morning class. "Why are you just sitting out here?" D.J. asked.

"I'm thinking," Stephanie told her. "About Alex."

"He's so cute," D.J. said. "I can tell you like him a lot."

"That's what I was afraid of." Stephanie sighed. "Deej, he's Darcy's boyfriend."

D.J. grimaced. "Ouch." She paused. "This is messy," she said. "Because I could tell he likes you, too."

"I think he does," Stephanie agreed. "D.J., what am I going to do?"

"I don't know," D.J. said. "That's a tough question."

"Did anything like this ever happen to you?" Stephanie asked.

"Once," D.J. replied. "It was terrible. The girl never spoke to me again. And I dated the guy for only a month before we broke up."

"Wow. So, you think I should forget about him?" Stephanie asked.

"Like I said, I don't know. Alex could be a passing thing, Steph," D.J. told her. "Or he could be the guy you love for the rest of your life. That's always the problem. You can't know how it's going to turn out."

"I wish I had a crystal ball!" Stephanie sighed.

D.J. nodded. "We all feel that way sometimes. Good luck. Let me know how it goes." With a wave, she headed down the street toward her bus stop.

Stephanie thought about D.J.'s words. She *didn't* know how things with Alex would turn out. But she had a feeling that she'd always be friends with Darcy. That kind of friendship was too precious to give up.

No matter how hard it was—or how much it hurt—she would never let herself be alone with Alex. Not ever again.

"But you *have to* come to the store with me!" Stephanie wailed.

Allie stared at her in surprise. She slammed her locker shut. "I'm sorry, Steph, but I forgot all about my piano lesson until this afternoon," Allie explained. "It's a special makeup session. Why the fuss? You'll have Alex to help you carry stuff."

Stephanie sighed. "I guess. At least Maura will be there," she added.

"No, afraid not," Allie told her. "Maura went home sick."

"What!" Stephanie shrieked.

"Yeah, she has a bad cold or something," Allie said. "Alex can help you if you want help and—"

Stephanie threw her arms wide in despair. "That's exactly what I *don't* want!" she blurted out.

"Why not?" Allie asked.

Stephanie realized she'd said too much. No one could know her secret, not even Allie. "Uh, because it feels wrong, asking him to do so much," she said, trying to cover up. "We'll have lots to carry."

Allie squinted at her suspiciously. "Did Alex upset you somehow?"

"No. Of course not," Stephanie said, turning away.

"Are you sure?" Allie probed.

"Absolutely," Stephanie insisted. "I'd better get going." With a wave, she turned and walked away. As she moved down the hall, she had the feeling Allie was still watching her. When she turned back to check, she was right.

Turning the hall corner, she stopped short. "Darcy!" she cried. She'd nearly walked right into her.

"Hi, stranger," Darcy said, smiling.

"Why did you call me that?" Stephanie asked.

"I just haven't seen much of you lately, now that I have soccer practice in the afternoons," Darcy answered. "Where are you headed now?"

"Uh . . . home," Stephanie replied.

"I'll walk with you," Darcy offered. Stephanie began walking again, and Darcy fell into step beside her. "Alex told me you guys run great together. Are you enjoying it?"

Stephanie hoped there was no look on her face to betray how guilty she felt. "Yeah," she said. "It's okay. I mean, it's fun."

"You are such a pal to do this for me," Darcy went on. "Not many people would get up at dawn to jog with a guy they hardly know."

"I don't mind," Stephanie said.

"What have you been doing lately?" Darcy asked. "It's like you and Maura and Allie disappear in the afternoons."

"You know. Lessons, clubs, that sort of thing." Stephanie gazed at the floor as they walked.

"I guess I'm just being paranoid," Darcy said. "I've had this weird feeling that something's going on with all of you."

"What could be going on?" Stephanie forced a laugh. "That's crazy."

"Yeah, I guess it is." Darcy grabbed hold of

Stephanie's arm and squeezed it affectionately. "You guys are the greatest friends anyone could have."

"Thanks," Stephanie replied.

"Want to watch my soccer practice today?" Darcy asked.

"Can't," Stephanie told her. "Big math test tomorrow. Got to study."

"Too bad," Darcy sympathized.

Stephanie nodded. "We'll do something together soon. I promise."

"Great!" Darcy said. She hesitated. "Well, I'd better get to my locker.'

"Okay. Bye." Stephanie watched Darcy turn and walk back in the direction of her locker. Darcy *was* the best. How could she even think of hurting her?

She couldn't, wouldn't. Losing her friendship was too high a price to pay for any boy.

She sighed. The trouble was, Alex wasn't just *any* boy. He was . . . Alex.

CHAPTER
7

◆ ◀ ✦ ◆

Stephanie spotted Alex standing in front of the party store, looking cuter than ever. The promises she'd made to herself instantly vanished. Her heart raced. She liked him so much!

She couldn't help feeling happy to see him.

The store was a large corner building with a huge plate-glass window on a busy street. Alex stood under the red awning in front. He turned and checked his reflection in the glass and smoothed his hair.

Stephanie smiled. He cared how he looked for her. He *did* like her—maybe as much as she liked him.

Stop! she scolded herself. *Don't be so happy to see him! Be normal!*

She drew in a deep breath to steady herself, then walked up to him. "Hi!"

Alex had been looking in the other direction. Startled, he jumped back slightly. "Oh! Hi." He smiled at her and she felt her heart do a flip of excitement.

"Ready to party-shop?" she asked.

"Ready," he replied.

They hurried inside. Stephanie studied the signs hanging from the ceiling. "That's it!" she said, pointing to one. "Mexican Fiesta."

Walking briskly, she headed toward the Mexican aisles. "Wow! Look at all this great stuff!" she said. There were chili-pepper lights, donkey-shaped piñatas, fiesta-colored plastic cups, a paper-cactus centerpiece.

"I don't know where to start," she said, looking around. "We'll need plates, napkins, and cups. Decorations, too, of course. Do you think red streamers are good?"

When he didn't say anything, she turned to look for him. He stepped forward, wearing a huge sombrero. He was wrapped in a brightly striped Mexican shawl.

"Senorita, I am the Mexican party expert! I

come to assist you," he joked in an awful version of a Mexican accent.

Stephanie cracked up. "Stop that!" she laughed, pulling the sombrero off his head.

"What? You do not want my expert assistance?" he said.

"Be serious," she scolded.

Alex continued clowning as they went up and down the aisle. "You're no help at all," she said with a smile, piling strings of chili lights into her shopping basket.

"But I'm the party expert, senorita. Remember?" he teased.

Stephanie turned a corner and froze. At the other end of the aisle, Darcy was shopping with her mother. They were searching in the bridal shower section. Stephanie suddenly remembered Darcy talking about a shower that her mother was giving for an old friend.

She felt a burst of panic and clutched Alex's sleeve. "It's Darcy!" she blurted out. "Hide!"

She pulled him back up the aisle, behind a life-sized cardboard cutout of a mariachi band—three Mexican men playing instruments, dressed in fancy, embroidered costumes and large straw sombreros.

"What are you doing?" Alex asked.

"She can't see us together," Stephanie said without thinking. "She'll think something's going on!"

Alex regarded her silently for a moment. "She'd be right," he finally said in a quiet voice. "Something *is* going on."

His words made Stephanie's heart pound. What did *he* think was going on between them?

"The *party* is going on," he added. "We don't want to ruin the surprise."

"Oh . . . the party . . . r-right," Stephanie sputtered. "Of course, we have to keep it a surprise."

"Right. Darcy doesn't know a thing about it," Alex said.

"And that's why we had to hide," Stephanie added. "If she saw us buying party stuff, she'd guess."

Stephanie knew she wasn't thinking about the party at all. She was actually feeling guilty about her crush.

But I haven't done anything about it, she reminded herself. *I have no intention of doing anything about it.*

"Say cheese!"

"Oh, no!" Stephanie jumped and stumbled in the narrow space. Her sudden movement was enough to throw Alex off balance. They both toppled backward into a huge bin stuffed with plastic lanterns.

"Ouch!" Stephanie exclaimed. Michelle stood over her, aiming her camera at Stephanie's startled face.

Snap!

"Excellent picture!" Michelle declared. She snapped away as Stephanie and Alex struggled to get out of the bin.

"Michelle, what are you doing here?" Stephanie demanded.

"I'm with Mandy and her mom," Michelle explained. Mandy Metz was Michelle's best friend. "We're shopping for Mandy's birthday party. Lucky I brought my camera, huh? Could you just move a little closer to Alex? I can't fit both of you in the shot, and this will make a great picture."

"Get out of here!" Stephanie told her.

"Yeah, no more pictures, please," Alex seconded.

"Fine, be that way!" Michelle sulked as she walked away.

Stephanie shook her head. "Can we get out of here now?" Alex whispered.

"Not yet," Stephanie warned. "What if we run into Darcy again?"

Stephanie peeked around the mariachi band cutout. She saw Darcy and Mrs. Powell cross the aisle and head toward the cash registers.

"They went to pay," Stephanie whispered to Alex. "They'll be gone in a minute."

"I'm getting up," Alex said. He made it halfway to his feet, then slipped and knocked over the mariachi band.

He and Stephanie both burst out laughing.

"I can't believe this," Alex said. He reached out and grabbed Stephanie's hand.

"What are you doing?" she asked.

"Helping you up," Alex said. He pulled her gently toward him.

Stephanie found herself standing about two inches away from him. She ignored the way her pulse started racing. "Now what?" she asked in a weak voice.

"Now you help me carry these mariachi guys to the cash register," Alex said. "We've bonded. We're paying for them and taking them with us. Let's go."

Stephanie grinned as she followed him up the aisle.

"Michelle, don't be mad," Stephanie said. It was after dinner, and she and Michelle had just cleared the table together.

Michelle hadn't taken one picture all night. She also hadn't looked at Stephanie or spoken to her once.

"I didn't mean to upset you in the store," Stephanie said. "It's just that every time I turn around these days, there you are, snapping a photograph. It gets annoying, you know."

Michelle gazed at her with an expression of hurt pride. She opened her mouth to speak, but then changed her mind. Lifting her chin, she stomped out of the kitchen.

Stephanie sighed.

Someone cleared a throat behind her. She turned and saw Danny. "Steph, couldn't you be nicer to Michelle about this project?" he asked. He pulled out a kitchen chair and sat. "She picked you for her subject because she admires you."

"I know, Dad, but it's incredibly annoying. She never leaves me alone," Stephanie defended herself.

"It's just a few more days," Danny said. "She told me what happened today. You didn't have to be rude to her."

"I can't help it, Dad," Stephanie said. "She really bugs me."

"She doesn't mean to be annoying," Danny said. He stood and placed a hand on each of her shoulders. "Try to remember how you felt at her age," he suggested. "How important a school project seemed. I think that's all it will take."

Stephanie nodded as her dad walked out of the

kitchen. Why *was* Michelle's project annoying her so much? she wondered.

The answer came instantly.

She was the most annoyed when Alex was around.

Having her picture taken with him made her feel more guilty than ever—as if she were caught doing something she shouldn't be doing.

"But I'm not doing anything," she muttered.

Except stealing your best friend's boyfriend, her conscience replied.

I can't help it! she suddenly realized with a shock. *I like Alex—and he likes me back. It's no one's fault. It just happened.*

She thought of how comic Alex looked, carrying the mariachi band cutout out of the store. She burst into a wide smile.

He was just too cute. She couldn't help it. She liked him. And she couldn't stop.

CHAPTER
8

◆ ◀ ◆ ◆

Friday morning, Stephanie thought as she opened her eyes. *This is my last run with Alex.* She sat up and slapped off the alarm clock.

The next day was the track meet. Then she wouldn't have a reason to run with him anymore.

She sat forward in bed, hugging her pillow. After that morning, they'd have no more reason to be alone together. They still had the party to throw, but it wouldn't be the same. She'd never have him all to herself again.

The idea filled her with sadness.

But I have today, she thought. She jumped out of bed, grabbed her hairbrush from her bedside table, and began stroking her hair until it gleamed.

"Are you getting all fixed up to run again?" Michelle yawned and sat up in her bed.

Stephanie ignored the rush of annoyance that ran through her. She was trying to be friends with Michelle again. She didn't want to spoil that.

"Why not?" she said. "I always care about how I look." *Especially when I'm going to see Alex*, she added to herself.

"Why don't you go back to sleep?" she asked Michelle. "It's so early."

"I don't mind," Michelle said, getting out of bed. She followed Stephanie with her camera, snapping as she put on mascara and applied lip gloss. "Do you really need lip gloss to run?" she asked.

Stephanie pushed back another surge of annoyance. "My lips get chapped," she explained.

The night before she had made a silent promise not to fix her hair or put on makeup that morning. What was the point? She might like Alex, but she couldn't have him. She couldn't break Darcy's heart.

Still, the idea of letting Alex see her looking a mess was more than she could stand.

Michelle yawned again. She put her camera

down. "You're right, Stephanie," Michelle said. "It *is* early. I'm going back to bed."

Stephanie hid her smile. "Okay," she said. "See you later."

But being on her own didn't help things. In a way, having Michelle around might have made it easier. She was uncomfortable being alone with Alex. It was terrible to be so close to him and not tell him how she felt.

"You're quiet today," Alex noted as they ran along Mission Street. It was the last and easiest part of their run, and the time they usually talked most.

"So are you," Stephanie replied. "Quiet, I mean."

"I know," he said. "I keep thinking how this is our last run together."

Did he feel as sad as she did? she wondered.

"I know" was all she could think of to say.

They continued to run side by side. Stephanie felt closer to him than ever before.

"Well, that's it," she announced as they returned to their starting point.

"You know, it doesn't have to be the end," Alex blurted out. "I was thinking. Just because the meet is tomorrow, we don't have to stop running together."

Stephanie inhaled deeply. She didn't know how

to reply. Part of her wanted to see him every morning—forever. But another part—the part that was loyal to Darcy—knew it was best not to see him again.

"Well, let's just see how it goes," she replied vaguely.

He stared at her for a moment. "Okay," he finally said. "See you this afternoon, then."

"Why?" she asked.

"Party planning, remember?" He grinned.

"Oh, right. Yeah, see you!" She waved good-bye, chewing on her lip. Maura and Allie just *had* to come over that afternoon. No way would she be alone with him again. No way!

No matter how desperately she wanted to be.

"I really am sick, you know," Maura complained with a sniffle. She grabbed another tissue and sneezed as she followed Stephanie into the living room that afternoon.

"I know. I figured that out when you weren't in school today. But I need you to be here," Stephanie replied. "Allie absolutely can't come over."

Maura collapsed onto the couch and blew her nose again. "Why can't she come?"

"She had to go to her grandmother's," Stephanie told her.

Maura sighed. "But why can't you meet with Alex alone?" she asked.

Stephanie stiffened. Did she want to explain? No. She definitely didn't. No one could ever know how she felt.

"Um, because we have to get this party going," she said. Which was totally true.

The bell rang and she let Alex in. He glanced at Maura, and she thought she saw a glimmer of disappointment on his face. "Alex, you know Maura, don't you?" she said.

"Sure. Darcy's friend. Hi," he greeted her. "Did Stephanie show you the Mexican decorations we bought? Totally funky!"

"Not yet," Stephanie jumped in. "Maura, you'll love them. This party will be such a fun blast, and—"

"*Mexican* decorations?" Maura blinked in surprise.

"Yeah, of course," Stephanie replied.

"Why do we need Mexican decorations for a dress-up party?" Maura asked.

"Dress-up party?" Stephanie looked at her in confusion.

"Sure. Isn't that what we agreed on?" Maura asked. "We said we'd serve Mexican chili and fancy desserts at a romantic, dress-up party."

"No," Stephanie answered. "I said we could serve romantic desserts at the *Mexican* party. The casual, fun Mexican party."

Maura scowled and crossed her arms. "That is not what I thought you meant."

"Well, it *is* what I meant," Stephanie replied. "I'm sure I was clear about it. We don't want a dress-up party."

"But Allie agreed with me," Maura insisted. "Obviously, you weren't listening."

"Me?" Stephanie cried.

"Yes, you. It doesn't matter, though. We'll just go ahead with the dress-up party. You serve chili. I know a great recipe for flan—a Spanish baked custard. It's perfect."

"But, Maura, Alex and I already bought a ton of Mexican decorations!" Stephanie protested.

"Yeah," Alex added. "I had to carry a whole mariachi band home!"

"Which is standing in my room at this very moment," Stephanie went on. "We also got chili lights, a paper cactus, matching chili-pepper paper plates, cups, and napkins, a dozen cheap sombreros, and a poster that says THIS WAY TO TIJUANA!"

"But I bought things, too," Maura argued. "I have a zillion little foil cups for the flan, ten pounds of chocolate, paper doilies, silk roses and little vases, and candles."

"How could you buy all that stuff without telling me?" Stephanie demanded.

"How could *you?*" Maura shot back, then sneezed.

"Listen, it's not a big deal," Alex broke in. "One of you will just return what you bought."

"Which one?" Maura and Stephanie asked in unison.

Alex shrugged. "I don't know."

After a long while, Stephanie spoke. "I will."

"Are you sure?" Maura asked.

"One of us has to," Stephanie said, feeling annoyed.

"Thanks," Maura said. "I'm too zoned out to return mine." She sneezed again and got up from the couch. "I'm sorry, but I really have to go. I shouldn't even be here in the first place."

"Okay," Stephanie said, walking with her to the door. "Maybe I'll see you in school tomorrow."

Maura left. Their argument left Stephanie feeling totally grouchy. She wished she'd never thought of a birthday party. Now that it would be a romantic party, it would be torture for her.

She'd have to watch Darcy and Alex, dancing and laughing together over a candlelit dinner. Being a couple, all night long.

"Let's just take that stuff back right now," Alex suggested.

"You'll have to carry the mariachi band all the way back again," Stephanie reminded him.

"Those guys don't scare me," Alex joked. "Bring them on."

Stephanie chuckled. Alex always made her feel better. Then she felt a stab of pain. *But he'll never be my boyfriend,* she thought.

"I'll get them from my room," she said, climbing the stairs.

An hour and a half later, they were back in her living room. "Thank goodness that's done," Stephanie said, flopping onto the couch.

Alex threw himself down beside her. Returning the party things with him really helped. It wasn't nearly as depressing and disappointing as it would have been to do it on her own.

"Now we have to shift gears and replan," she said. "Don't think Mexican anymore. Think romantic desserts."

Alex leaned closer to her. He gazed into her

eyes. "It's easy to think romantic thoughts when I'm with you," he said.

Stephanie swallowed hard. *What is he doing?* she wondered.

"Since I met you, I hardly think about Darcy at all," Alex admitted. "Only you."

"But I—" Before she could say more, he was kissing her.

CHAPTER
9

◆ ◀ ✦ ◆

I'll stop him—right now, Stephanie thought. But she didn't. Kissing Alex was really nice!

Something clicked in her ear.

"Michelle!" she shouted, pulling away from Alex.

Michelle had popped up from behind the couch. She grinned at Stephanie and snapped another picture.

"What have you done?" Stephanie shrieked. She'd just kissed her best friend's boyfriend. And her little sister had a photo of her doing it!

She felt a burst of panic. "Alex, you have to go," she said. She grabbed his arm and steered him toward the front door. "I can't deal with this right now."

"You're not upset, are you?" he asked.

"No. I just have to think." She yanked the door open and nearly pushed him onto the stoop.

"Stephanie, hold on. We have to talk about this," he pleaded. "Listen, I know you feel the same about me as I feel about —"

"I really can't talk now," she cut him off. "I need time to think. Really. Please."

He looked at her for a moment. "I'll see you tomorrow, won't I? At the track meet?"

"Sure," she replied. "I wouldn't miss that. See you then."

He smiled, but she couldn't even look at him. "Okay. I'll see you tomorrow," he said as he left.

She started to run up the stairs to her room.

"Steph—are you mad at me again?" Michelle called after her.

"No. Yes. I don't know!" Stephanie snapped. "Just leave me alone, Michelle!"

In her room, she slammed the door and threw herself facedown on her bed. She grabbed her pillow and pulled it over her head.

She was crazy about Alex! And now she knew he felt the same way about her.

Of all the boys on earth, why did she have to pick Darcy's boyfriend?

You tried to fight it, she told herself.

No, this was all her fault. Wasn't it? Had she led him on? Did he kiss her because he could tell she liked him?

Or would he have liked her anyway, even if she hadn't liked him first?

When dinnertime came, she said she had a stomachache and didn't want to eat. Danny came up with a tray of food and some medicine. "Is there anything you want to talk about?" he asked.

"No, I just don't feel so good," she said. "Thanks."

When she finally drifted off to sleep that night, she dreamed she was walking with Darcy. Darcy wouldn't speak to her. She only gazed at her with hurt, accusing eyes.

She awoke on Saturday and was filled with dread. How could she watch the track meet? She wanted John Muir to win, but she couldn't go. Darcy would be there.

How can I face her? she wondered. *And how can I stand to see her with Alex?*

Michelle woke up and stretched.

"Hey, Michelle—want to come to the track meet with me?" she asked. "You can take photos of every single thing that goes on."

"No way," Michelle replied. "I'm done with photographs. I'm all worn out."

"But it hasn't been a full week," Stephanie pointed out.

"I told my teacher I was having trouble with my subject," Michelle said. "She said to cut it short. So I did."

"Michelle, I'm sorry I snapped at you yesterday," Stephanie began. "But . . . you surprised me."

"I'm sorry, too," Michelle replied. "I didn't realize you two were all kissy-face until it was too late."

"We weren't kissy-face!" Stephanie cried.

"Really? What do you call it?" Michelle asked.

"Okay, so Alex kissed me," Stephanie admitted. "But I didn't kiss him back. At least, I didn't mean to. It all happened so fast, I didn't know what I was doing."

"Whatever," Michelle said with a shrug. "I still can't go to the track meet. Dad's taking me to the one-hour photo place in the mall. I'm having my film developed today."

"Okay," Stephanie said, giving up.

She dressed, ate a quick breakfast, and headed over to school. Their rivals from Jefferson Middle School had already arrived. The parking lot was crowded with kids and families moving toward the track from all directions.

"Stephanie!" She recognized Allie's voice and turned. Allie and Darcy were hurrying across the lot toward her.

"Aren't you psyched?" Darcy asked. "We can both feel like we did our part if John Muir wins today."

"What you mean, if?" Allie teased. "We're a cinch to win!"

Darcy wrapped her arm around Stephanie's shoulders. "Thanks again for running with Alex," she said. "I know it wasn't easy, getting up so early."

"It wasn't as bad as I expected," Stephanie replied. She forced a smile. She wished she felt the same eager excitement as Allie and Darcy. But all she wanted was to go home. She dreaded seeing Alex.

The meet was about to start, so they moved into the bleachers closest to the track. Stephanie spotted Alex with his teammates, but he didn't notice her. He looked serious, with an intense expression of concentration.

"Look how focused he is," Darcy said to Stephanie. "Right now he's not thinking about anything else on earth except getting a fast start."

Stephanie looked hard at Darcy. It was clear from her tone that Darcy thought she and Alex were as close as two people could be.

But she was wrong. Alex had told Stephanie so himself. Stephanie felt terrible. When Darcy found out how Alex really felt, she'd be totally crushed.

The meet began. Stephanie cheered along with Allie, Darcy, and the rest of the John Muir crowd.

Alex fell behind in the first race. She clenched her fists together. What was the matter? "Go, Alex!" she screamed.

Darcy turned to her. "Don't worry," she said. "Sometimes he starts slow. He'll make up for it later."

"Really?" *How can she be so calm?* Stephanie wondered.

A thought popped into her head. Maybe Darcy didn't care about Alex as much as she did. She didn't look very concerned right now. After all, he was in fourth place, and she was perfectly calm.

"Go, Alex!" Stephanie yelled again. "Go! Go! Go!"

Darcy nudged her in the side. "Watch him now," she said.

As if he'd heard her, Alex put on a burst of speed. He passed the boy in front of him and then the next one. With astonishing smoothness he passed every other runner. In a moment, he was well ahead of everyone.

"Yes!" Darcy cheered, pumping the air. "Go, Alex, go!" Her eyes were bright with pride as Alex crossed the finish line first. "That's my guy!" she shouted. "I knew he could do it."

Stephanie's image of an uncaring Darcy vanished. The look on her face said it all. She was still crazy about him.

The rest of the meet was close. But Alex won race after race. Thanks to him, John Muir won. They were the new regional champions.

And Alex was a star.

As he left the track, he was mobbed by crowds of cheering kids.

"Come on," Darcy said, tugging Stephanie's arm. "Let's go see him."

"Uh, you go," Stephanie said. "You're his girl-friend."

"Don't be silly," Darcy told her. "You were his co-runner! You're important to him, too."

"Are you coming, Allie?" Stephanie asked.

"Sure." Allie tagged along as Darcy pulled Stephanie down the bleachers. She was so fired with enthusiasm that she didn't notice Stephanie's dragging feet. With Darcy in the lead, they wriggled their way through the crowd until they reached Alex.

He was being interviewed by a reporter from a

small newspaper that covered local events. "Here they are—my assistant trainers," Alex joked to the reporter.

The reporter turned to the woman beside him, a photographer. "Let's get a picture of all three of them," he said.

"Oh, no," Stephanie protested, stepping back. "Not me."

"Come on," Darcy insisted, pulling her forward.

Stephanie shot a look at Alex. He seemed perfectly comfortable with the situation. In fact, he smiled and put an arm around each of them. Darcy smiled in excitement, standing on his right.

Stephanie stood on his left. She forced the corners of her mouth into a smile, but she was sure it wasn't convincing. This was about as awful a moment as she could ever have imagined.

Alex stood between the two of them, acting totally happy. How could he be so relaxed? Stephanie felt as if she'd burst with the weight of their secret. Poor Darcy! She had no idea what was *really* going on!

Then she remembered what Darcy said—Alex could focus on one thing at a time. Maybe he was still in that frame of mind. He was thinking of them only as the two joggers who had helped him train for his big victory.

But *she* wasn't like that.

"Smile!" the photographer called as she took her shot.

"Okay. I have to go now," Stephanie said, pulling away from Alex. She made her way through the crowd back to the bleachers. She didn't look back.

She felt suddenly sick to her stomach. She collapsed on the first row of bleachers, dropping her face into her hands.

"What's wrong, Steph?" Allie's voice asked. "Are you sick?" Stephanie looked up as Allie sat beside her. "Oh, Allie! Everything is horrible!" she blurted out.

"What's horrible?" Allie asked.

Stephanie lowered her voice. "It's Alex," she admitted. "I think . . . I mean, I'm sure . . ." She paused.

"That you like him," Allie finished quietly.

Stephanie stared at her in shock. "You knew? How could you tell?"

"It wasn't that hard," Allie said. "Your eyes get all sparkly whenever you say his name. You're always staring at him when you think no one's looking. And then there was the way you panicked when you had to be alone with him at the party store."

Stephanie groaned. "Do you think Darcy knows?"

Allie shook her head. "I'm pretty certain she doesn't. She's never said anything to me. And she was really happy that you went running with him."

"This is so terrible, Al," Stephanie said. She took a deep breath. "Because he likes me, too. He told me so."

"Wow. That *is* bad," Allie agreed.

Stephanie let her head drop in despair. "What am I going to do? I like him so much. I really do."

Allie sighed. "Do you like him enough to break Darcy's heart?"

CHAPTER
10

◆ ◀ ✦ ◆

Stephanie couldn't get comfortable. She crossed her legs. She uncrossed her legs. She dropped her feet onto the floor, then kicked them back up onto the sofa. She clicked on the TV, then clicked it off.

I can't make my thoughts comfortable, either, she admitted. *Any way I look at this problem, I lose.*

She could give up Alex completely. Tell him she refused to see him or even speak to him again.

But every time she thought of doing that, she felt an awful ache in her stomach. How could she stand it?

Besides, she would *have* to see him again—because he'd be with Darcy!

Face it, she told herself. *You have to tell Darcy the truth!* She cringed. The idea was too terrible. Darcy trusted her. She couldn't betray her best friend so completely. How could she even look at herself in the mirror again? She'd see the biggest creep who ever lived!

The phone rang. Stephanie let it ring, hoping someone else would get it. But no one did.

Becky was upstairs giving the twins their Saturday afternoon bath. D.J. was studying with friends at her college. Everyone else was in Golden Gate Park, having fun.

The phone machine clicked on. Stephanie listened as the family greeting played. Then it was time for the caller to leave a message.

"I'm calling for Stephanie," Alex's voice declared. "What happened to you? Where did you disappear to? You should have come out to celebrate with the rest of us. When you get this message, call me back. In case you don't have it, my number is —"

Stephanie leaped off the couch and snapped up the phone. "Hello?" she said breathlessly.

"Steph, hi!" Alex responded. "Did you hear my message?"

"Yeah." She swallowed. "I left because . . ."

"Was it because of Darcy?" he interrupted.

"Sort of," she admitted. *Totally*, she added to herself.

"I know," Alex said in a quiet voice. "It was a little weird, wasn't it?"

There was an uncomfortable pause. Then they both spoke at once. "We have to do something . . . !"

Alex laughed. "I know exactly what to do," he said. "I'm going to break up with Darcy."

"No!" Stephanie cried. "You can't!"

"What do you mean?" Alex sounded confused.

"You just can't. Please, don't," Stephanie begged. The churning feeling began in her stomach again.

"I don't get it," he said. "You *want* me to keep going out with her?"

"No, I don't," Stephanie replied. "But breaking up with her will hurt her so much. And her birthday is next week. I just can't do this to her now."

"What else can I do?" he demanded.

"Wait," Stephanie told him. "Wait until after her birthday."

"What difference would that make?" Alex challenged. "She'll still be upset."

He was right, Stephanie knew. The breakup would hurt Darcy as much after her birthday as it would now. But at least she'd have a happy birthday first.

Besides, waiting would give Stephanie more time to think about how Alex should break the awful news.

Plus, I'm a coward, she added to herself.

"I just think waiting is for the best. Let's not ruin her birthday," Stephanie told Alex. "At least she can enjoy her party."

Alex sighed. "If you think that's best, I'll wait," he said. "Though I'd rather get it over with now."

Becky appeared on the stairs with the twins. The boys looked fresh and clean in their terry cloth robes. They scampered down the stairs, heading toward the living room.

"Listen, Alex, I have to go," Stephanie said into the phone.

"Okay, I'll call you later," Alex replied.

"No, don't!" she exclaimed. "Um, I mean, I'll be out later." It wasn't true, but she just couldn't talk to Alex about Darcy anymore. She was too confused.

"Okay." Alex hung up.

The twins rushed at Stephanie. Nicky climbed onto the couch and gave her a hug. Alex plopped down next to her.

"Cousin Stephie, can you play with us?" Nicky asked.

Becky smoothed Nicky's damp hair. "Sorry, Steph—did we interrupt your phone call?"

"That's okay," Stephanie said.

"Well, I need to ask a big favor," Becky replied.

"What is it?" Stephanie asked.

"Could you watch the twins for a while?" Becky said. "The TV station just called. They need me to come down to see a tape segment for Monday's show. There's some problem with the sound track. I may need to write a new introduction and record it."

"Sure, I don't mind," Stephanie quickly agreed. Taking care of the boys would keep her from thinking about Alex and Darcy all day.

And that was the last thing she wanted to do.

"Thanks, Steph! You're a lifesaver," Becky told her. She gave Stephanie some last-minute instructions, then hurried out of the house.

"Okay, you guys," Stephanie told the twins. "Time to find some play clothes."

"Because we're going to play a *lot*, right?" Nicky asked.

"Right." Stephanie grinned.

The boys were a handful. Still, the time seemed to drag all afternoon. Stephanie played game after game. Hide-and-seek, car races, and finally a long game of catch in the backyard.

The whole time, part of her was hoping Alex would call back despite what she said. When

Becky finally came home, she took a long bike ride. Somehow, she made it through dinner.

She even went to bed early. But she couldn't fall asleep. Instead, she spent hours tossing and turning. Finally, she fell asleep and didn't wake up until late Sunday morning.

Pulling on jeans and a shirt, she headed downstairs. She passed Danny. He was on his way to his upstairs study.

"Morning, sleepyhead," Danny greeted her. "I left pancakes warming in the oven for you."

"Thanks, Dad," she replied. "But I'm not hungry."

"Are you feeling all right?" Danny reached out to press a hand against her forehead.

"I'm not sick," Stephanie told him. "Just a little bit down."

"Well, let me know if I can help," he told her.

"Sure," Stephanie replied. *No one can help*, she told herself, feeling gloomy.

She crossed the living room. Michelle sat on the couch, flipping through a stack of photos. "Are those the pictures for your big project?" she asked.

Michelle nodded. "Yeah. I got lots of cool shots. I bet I'll get a good grade on this."

Stephanie perched on the arm of the couch. "Can I see?"

Michelle handed her a stack of photos. Stephanie flipped through them. Some of them made her cringe—like the one where she was trying to hose down Comet. Her face was all squished up, and her hair was wet and stringy.

There was another shot of her taking out the trash. Michelle had taken it from the back porch, aiming the camera down at Stephanie. The odd angle made Stephanie's legs look incredibly short and squat.

"Ugh, Michelle," she said. "I look awful in some of these."

"I can't help that," Michelle told her. "It was a big job, recording everything you did this week. I couldn't worry about how you looked, too."

"Well, I guess no one will see these but your class," Stephanie reasoned. "Maybe it doesn't matter."

She flipped another photo over. *Oh, no!*

She stared at a shot of Alex and her falling into the bin at the party store.

She flipped the next photo. Alex kissing her!

She snatched the photo and lifted it out of Michelle's reach. "Michelle, you are *not* using this picture," she cried. "No way!"

"I have to!" Michelle protested. "That's one of my best shots."

"No. Absolutely *no*!" Stephanie exclaimed.

Michelle jumped at her, trying to grab the photo back. "Give it to me!" she demanded.

"In your dreams!" Stephanie told her.

Michelle kept jumping. "I mean it, Stephanie!" she declared. "That's part of my project. It belongs to me!"

Stephanie backed away from her. She turned, scanning the living room. She spotted the high shelf near the front door. She ran over and reached up on tiptoe. She slipped the photo onto the shelf. "There!" she said. "It's safe now."

"No fair!" Michelle cried. She darted into the kitchen and returned, dragging the step stool.

"Don't you dare take that photo," Stephanie warned her. She planted herself in Michelle's path.

"Get out of my way!" Michelle demanded.

A door slammed upstairs. Danny appeared in the hallway. "What's going on down there?" he demanded. "It's so noisy, I can't work!"

"Stephanie stole one of my pictures!" Michelle shouted. "And she won't give it back!"

"I don't want her to use it," Stephanie explained. "It's a picture of me, and it's really, really embarrassing!"

"Michelle, I think Stephanie should have some

say about what pictures you use and don't use," Danny said, taking Stephanie's side.

Michelle jutted out her lower lip. "I don't think that's very fair," she protested. "I worked hard taking these shots."

"It's only one picture," Danny pointed out. "If it upsets Stephanie this much, I think you can do without it."

"Oh, okay," Michelle muttered. "But that's the only one. I'm using all the rest."

"Fine," Stephanie snapped.

"Fine!" Michelle snapped back.

The doorbell rang. "I'll get it." Stephanie reached out and pulled open the door.

Darcy stood on the front step.

"Darcy! Hi," Stephanie greeted her in surprise. "I didn't expect you."

"I know," Darcy replied, stepping inside. "Sorry I didn't call. I didn't plan to come by. But I was walking past your street—and I just have to talk to you!"

A feeling of dread filled Stephanie's stomach. She licked her lips. "Talk to me? About what?" she asked, trying to sound casual.

"I finally figured it out," Darcy stated. "I'm not paranoid. There is something going on. And I know what!"

CHAPTER
11

◆ ◂ ⬩ ◆

Stephanie's heart slammed hard in her chest. She turned pale. Her palms got sweaty.

Darcy knew!

Her mind raced. *Who told? Allie? No. She wouldn't.*

Alex! Alex called her and broke up with her!

"I feel really bad about what I'm going to say next," Darcy began. "So first, let me say I'm really sorry."

"Sorry? For what?" Stephanie stared at her in confusion.

"For being so gone over Alex," Darcy replied. "So gone that I barely paid attention to my own best friends."

"Oh," Stephanie said, feeling instant relief. Then Darcy *didn't* know about her and Alex!

"I always hate it when girls go gaga over some guy," Darcy went on. "You know, they ignore their friends. They don't think of anything else but him." Darcy shook her head in disgust. "I always thought it was so dumb to make a guy the center of your universe. And I did the same thing! I can't help it when it comes to Alex."

"Well, uh . . . uh . . ." Stephanie stammered.

Darcy grinned and shook her head. "Then I put two and two together," she went on. "You guys are throwing me a surprise party, aren't you?"

"Well . . ." Stephanie began.

"You don't have to tell me," Darcy stopped her. "I guessed, okay? But you've been avoiding me all week. And my birthday is coming up. It isn't that hard to figure out."

"I, uh . . . I don't know what to say," Stephanie replied.

"Don't say anything," Darcy said. "As long as you promise not to throw the party on Tuesday. Because I still really, really want to go out with Alex on my birthday night."

"Tuesday?" Stephanie repeated. "No problem. You don't have to worry about Tuesday night."

Darcy let out a deep whoosh of air. "Great. I'm so glad I brought it up. You don't know how worried I was about hurting your feelings. But it's out in the open now. Are you mad?"

"No!" Stephanie exclaimed. "I'm not mad. Not at all. I'm glad you told me. You should do whatever you want on your birthday night. It's *your* birthday, after all. Right? Right. Definitely right. Don't worry about a thing. There definitely won't be a party on Tuesday night!"

Darcy stared at her. "Why are you carrying on about it?"

"Uh, no reason," Stephanie said. "I'm just glad nobody's mad at anyone else."

"And I'm glad you understand how I feel," Darcy replied. She wrapped Stephanie in a giant hug. "You're just the best friend in the whole world."

The best friend in the world? Not quite, Stephanie thought. *Your best friend wouldn't be sneaking around with your boyfriend!*

Darcy had no idea what a scare she'd given her. *Thank goodness she didn't guess about me and Alex!* she told herself. She was flooded with relief.

And she'll never know, Stephanie suddenly vowed. *What was I thinking?* No way could she ever hurt Darcy.

She was going to call Alex and tell him it was

over. Nothing more could happen between them. She'd call him the minute Darcy left.

They could have the party for Darcy, and she'd never know the truth.

Somehow, Stephanie would make it through the night. And then she would avoid Alex completely. Totally. Until they both forgot about one another.

It would hurt, but she'd do it. And she'd do it right away. The sooner the better.

A car horn sounded outside. An instant later, D.J. flew down the stairs.

"Stephanie! Quick!" D.J. demanded. "My friends are here—and I can't find my literature textbook! I need to bring it to our study session today. Do you know where it is?"

"You put it right here, Deej," Stephanie told her. "Don't you remember?" She pointed to the shelf next to the door.

"Right!" D.J. cried happily. She scooped up the book and darted out the front door.

"Wow, college work sure must be demanding," Darcy noted. "Imagine working that hard on a Sunday!"

"D.J. is always working hard," Stephanie agreed.

Darcy nodded. "So, what are you doing now? Want to hang out for the rest of the day?"

"No! Um, actually, I have some work to do, too," Stephanie fibbed. *Like, calling Alex the minute you leave,* she thought.

"Okay. Then I'd better go and let you do it," Darcy said. She turned toward the door. "What kind of work, anyway? That history paper?"

"Yeah, that and some other odds and ends," Stephanie replied. She reached for the doorknob, hoping that Darcy would get the hint.

She froze.

A photograph lay facedown on the floor, right in front of the door.

The photo of her kissing Alex.

She inhaled a sharp breath. D.J. must have knocked the photo off the shelf when she grabbed her book. Thank goodness it had fallen upside down.

"So, Darce, I'm glad we settled this. Call me tonight!" she said, trying to herd Darcy out the door.

Too late.

Darcy had already noticed the photo on the floor. "What's this?" she asked. She stooped to pick it up.

"I guess it fell off the shelf," Stephanie told her. "It's nothing. I'll take it."

She reached to grab the photo before Darcy could take a look at it.

"Sure." Darcy went to hand her the photo. As she held it out, she turned the picture over.

And stared.

CHAPTER
12

♦ ◄ ✦ ♦

Darcy's eyes opened wide in shock. She stared down at the photo as if she couldn't quite believe what she was seeing.

Stephanie felt as though time stood still. As if she were stuck in a nightmare that would never end.

Slowly, Darcy tore her gaze away from the picture. She glanced up at Stephanie. There were tears in her eyes.

"What is this?" she asked.

"Darce, I can explain," Stephanie began. *Explain how? Explain what?* she thought wildly.

"I'm listening," Darcy said in a small, tight voice.

Stephanie felt the blood rush to her face. Her cheeks burned. "I didn't mean for it to happen," she said. Her own voice was so small, she could barely hear it.

"Then, this is for real?" Darcy demanded. "It's not some terrible joke? This is really you and Alex—kissing?"

Stephanie nodded.

Darcy's eyes squeezed shut. She bit her lip. Then she crumpled the photo in her fist. "How could you?" she demanded. "How could you do this to me?"

"Darcy, please," Stephanie pleaded. "It's not what you think. It . . . it just happened."

"Oh, really?" Darcy gave a scornful laugh. "You and Alex just happened to be sneaking around behind my back?"

"It wasn't like that!" Stephanie exclaimed. "Not at first."

"Oh, great!" Darcy spat out. "So, you've been sneaking around only *lately*?"

"We didn't mean to sneak around at all!" Stephanie tried to explain. "Honestly, it just happened, Darce. We just started to like each other. I feel terrible about it. I'd do anything to change things. I already promised myself I'd never see him again!"

"It's a little late for that, isn't it?" Darcy said.

"I guess so," Stephanie mumbled. "I'm so sorry, Darcy."

"Not as sorry as I am," Darcy replied. "I can't believe my best friend would stab me in the back this way. And right before my birthday, too!"

"Darcy, really, I—"

Darcy threw the crumpled photo at Stephanie. She whirled and marched away, storming out of the house and slamming the front door behind her.

Bang!

Stephanie jumped at the sound. And burst into tears. She collapsed onto the bottom step and wailed.

"Stephanie?" Her father slowly climbed down the stairs. "What's wrong, sweetheart?"

"Nothing. Everything!" she answered. Her stomach churned worse than ever. And she could feel a headache coming on.

"Maybe I should get you something," Danny said, heading for the kitchen. "A nice cup of tea."

"Sure, fine," Stephanie mumbled. How could tea make her feel better? How could anything?

The phone rang. What if it was Alex?

Worse—what if her dad answered?

She bolted to the living room phone and snatched it up. "Hello?" she asked.

"Steph, it's me, Allie!" Allie sounded totally calm. "I had a question about the party. I was wondering if—"

"The party! Forget the party," Stephanie cut her off.

"Huh." Allie asked. "What are you talking about?"

"Darcy. She knows—about me and Alex," Stephanie said.

Allie was silent on the other end.

"Say something!" Stephanie pleaded.

"When did it happen?" Allie asked.

"Just now. It was so terrible," Stephanie told her. Fresh tears filled her eyes. "She just dropped over my house. And she saw a picture of me and Alex . . . together."

"Together how?" Allie demanded.

"Kissing," Stephanie admitted.

"Oh, wow!" Allie cried. "This is really bad, Stephanie. Who took a picture like that, anyway?"

"Michelle."

"And Darcy saw it? Stephanie, how could you let that happen? How could you do that to her?" Allie cried.

Stephanie felt as if she'd been slapped. "It was an accident! You could be a little supportive," she told Allie. "I feel bad enough already."

"I'm sorry," Allie replied. "I guess the truth is, I just don't get any of this. I don't see what's so great about Alex. I never did."

Tears ran down Stephanie's cheeks. "I can't talk about this anymore," she told Allie. "I have to say good-bye." Without another word, she hung up.

Danny rushed into the living room with a cup of tea on a tray. "Here, Steph, honey. Maybe this will help," he said.

"Nothing will help." Stephanie brushed away tears. "I feel too terrible."

"Can't you tell me what happened?" he asked.

Stephanie stood. "Do you mind if we don't talk about it now? I just want to be alone."

"Sure," Danny told her. "But if you want to talk later, you know I'm here."

"Thanks." She hurried past him and raced up to her room. She threw herself on her bed.

This was the worst thing that ever happened to her. Darcy hated her. Allie couldn't understand what was going on.

And she was more confused than ever.

After a long cry, her tears finally stopped. She slowly wiped her eyes. Darcy would probably never forgive her. Stephanie drew her knees up to her chest and wrapped her arms around them.

She remembered her vow to break off with Alex. It was probably the right thing to do.

But then, everything was different now. She'd hurt Darcy. Their friendship was over.

Why should she lose Alex, too?

CHAPTER
13

◆ ◀ ◂ ◆

"What *happened?*" Maura asked Monday in school. "I went to Darcy's locker and she totally iced me out. When I asked her what was wrong, she just walked away."

Stephanie shut her locker and slumped back against it. "Oh, wow. She must think you were in on it all along. Allie, too. Otherwise she would have called you right away and told you what happened. That proves she thinks you and Allie knew."

"Knew what?" Maura asked. "What are you talking about?"

Stephanie quickly filled her in on what had happened—how she had a huge crush on Alex.

That Alex liked her back. And that Darcy found a photo of them kissing.

"You probably think I'm the biggest creep in the world," Stephanie finished.

Maura shook her head. "No, I don't blame you," she said. "You and Alex have been spending a lot of time together. And he is really cute. I can see how it might happen."

"Thanks for understanding, Maura," Stephanie said.

"So, are you going to keep seeing him?" Maura asked.

"I don't know," Stephanie admitted. "One minute, I think I won't. And then, the next minute, I think that I might as well."

"Maybe you should break up with him," Maura said. "Just to show Darcy how much you care about her friendship."

"I could," Stephanie said. "But the damage is already done. You know Darcy—she's so stubborn! She might not forgive me no matter what I do."

Maura sighed. "This is so complicated! I wish Darcy would talk to me. Then I could find out what you should do."

"Could you try again?" Stephanie pleaded. "I feel so awful about this."

"I'll try," Maura agreed. "But she must feel so

betrayed. Especially if she thinks all three of us went against her."

"I know," Stephanie agreed. She had never felt so miserable in her life.

"Hey—don't look now, but here comes Alex." Maura poked Stephanie in the side.

Stephanie glanced up as Alex rounded the corner and headed down the hall. Her heart gave a little *thump*. He was *so* cute! She couldn't help feeling a little burst of pride. He liked her. He was her boyfriend—almost.

"I'll let you two talk in private." Maura hurried away.

"Thanks," Stephanie murmured.

Alex saw her and broke into a wide grin. "Steph! How are you doing?" he greeted her.

She studied his expression. It was obvious he didn't know what happened with Darcy.

"I'm not doing so great," she told him. She swallowed hard. "Darcy saw the picture Michelle took of you kissing me."

"Ouch!" Alex cringed. "Did she freak?"

"Sort of. Yeah," Stephanie admitted.

Alex nodded. "Well, that's why I didn't like Michelle taking those pictures," he said. "I knew it would mean trouble."

"I guess you were right," she agreed.

"At least now Darcy knows about us," he said.

"Yeah. But it's terrible," Stephanie said. "She's my best friend, and I stabbed her in the back."

"True," Alex said. "But we knew she was going to be hurt sooner or later. It just happened sooner than we expected."

Stephanie studied his face in surprise. He didn't seem upset at all. His reaction unsettled her. It wasn't exactly cold—but he could have shown a little more concern.

"Don't you care that we hurt her?" she asked.

"Sure I care," he replied. "But there's nothing we can do about it now."

"I wish none of this ever happened," she said. "Everything just tumbled out of control—and then that stupid photo clinched it. I never wanted to hurt Darcy."

"Look, we didn't do anything wrong," Alex told her.

"Really?" Stephanie asked. "Then why do I feel so terrible?"

"Because it happened just yesterday," Alex replied. "In a week or two, she'll get over it. She'll probably even start seeing someone else. These things always work out."

"You sound like you've been through this before," Stephanie remarked.

He shrugged. "I've been through other breakups. So has Darcy. Hasn't she?"

"Yeah, I guess so," Stephanie replied. "But this is different. You broke up with her to go out with me—her best friend."

"That's just the way it worked out," Alex said. "Don't worry so much. Breaking up is always tough at first. But it all kind of works itself out."

"I guess you're right," she said slowly.

"Sure I am!" Alex grinned. "Don't let it get to you," he advised. "Now we can be a couple, out in the open. That's cool, right? Think about that."

She forced a small smile. "You're right. That's the good part."

"Sure it is," he agreed. "I'd better get to home-room." He waved as he walked off down the hall. "I'll call you later."

Stephanie watched him go. Everything he said made sense. Maybe he was right. Maybe she needed to give things more time. In time maybe her guilty feelings would go away.

She went through the rest of the morning feeling gloomy. She listened to her lessons in a half daze.

At lunch she met Maura and Allie, as usual. Darcy sat with some girls from the soccer team.

Stephanie felt a pang of misery. "I can't stand this," she told her friends. "Darcy won't even look at us."

"It's pretty terrible," Maura agreed.

Allie sighed. "If only Darcy had gone out with Ben instead of with Alex," she said, "none of this would have happened. Ben would never have broken her heart like that creep Alex."

"Alex isn't a creep," Stephanie protested.

Allie reddened. "Sorry, Steph," she said. "I know you like him. But I just can't quite trust him."

"Lighten up, Allie," Maura said. "Stephanie feels bad enough already."

"Oops. Sorry again," Allie replied. "Really, Steph. I don't want you to feel bad. At least you have Alex now."

"Yeah. I should be glad about that," Stephanie replied. "But I feel so bad about what we did to Darcy. I can't feel happy about anything else."

"Imagine how Darcy must feel," Allie said.

"Allie!" Maura warned.

"I'm sorry," Allie protested. "But I have to tell it like I see it."

"Allie's right," Stephanie added. "I caused Darcy a lot of hurt."

She stared down at her hot lunch. It was chicken and mashed potatoes, one of the more edible school lunches, but she couldn't eat a bite. Her appetite had completely disappeared.

"Stephanie, you look miserable," Maura noted. "I know! Why don't we go to the movies tonight? That should take your mind off your problems. We can't do anything for Darcy—at least not until she'll talk to us. But we can try to cheer you up."

"That sounds good," Stephanie agreed. Two hours of total escape.

They agreed to meet at Stephanie's house at six. For the rest of lunch, they debated what movie to see.

This isn't so bad, Stephanie told herself. *I just have to force myself not to look at Darcy. I almost feel like my old self again!*

"Oh, no! Look at the line!" Stephanie exclaimed.

She stopped short as they came in sight of the movie theater in the mall. The line reached from the theater, past the health food store, past the jewelry store, the computer software store, and out to the fountain.

"It's probably for the new Disney movie," Maura said. "It just came out." She gestured toward all the little kids waiting on line with their parents.

111

"Right," Allie added. "There should be plenty of tickets for our movie."

They took their places at the end of the line. Allie began chatting about the star of the film they were going to see. "Parker Smith is completely adorable," she declared. "But he's not very funny."

"How can you say that?" Maura demanded. "I think he's a great comedy actor!"

Stephanie barely paid attention to the conversation. The only thing on her mind was Darcy and Alex. And she was forbidden to talk about that. It was difficult to think about anything else.

The line crept along slowly. Soon Allie and Maura ran out of topics to discuss. Stephanie guessed they were thinking about Darcy and Alex, too. They all fell into an awkward silence.

"Maybe I should buy us all popcorn," Stephanie remarked. She turned to go toward the snack bar and caught sight of a familiar-looking figure outside in the courtyard.

"Alex!" she murmured. Was it him? The boy was standing in the doorway of the jewelry store. She never saw Alex wear a black denim jacket before. Still, she was pretty sure it was him. She craned her neck to get a better look.

"I think I see Alex over there," she told her friends.

"Really? I wonder what he's doing here," Allie asked.

"Maybe he's upset, too," Stephanie said. "Maybe he came to the mall to clear his mind. I'm going to go say hi."

"Okay, but come right back," Allie told her.

Stephanie hurried closer to the jewelry store. She was only a yard or so away, when the boy threw his head back, laughing.

It's definitely Alex, Stephanie told herself. *I wonder if he's here because he's upset about Darcy, too.*

At that moment, Alex took a step to one side.

Stephanie gasped. Alex wasn't alone. He leaned over a petite, pretty girl with bright red hair.

The next moment, Stephanie realized exactly what he was doing.

He was putting his arms around the pretty girl. And he was kissing her.

CHAPTER
14

◆ ◀ ◆ ◆

Stephanie staggered back. She felt as if someone had thrown a basketball at her stomach, full force. She felt as if all the air was just knocked out of her.

What should I do? she thought. *I can't let him see me!*

She darted into the doorway of the computer store. She leaned forward with her hands on her knees and swallowed great gulps of air.

Allie and Maura spotted her and rushed over. Allie placed a hand on her shoulder. "Are you okay?"

"You're totally pale," Maura said. "Put your head down."

Stephanie bent her head forward. In a minute her breathing was normal again.

"That Alex!" Allie exclaimed. "What a rat!"

"I think we saw what you saw," Maura told Stephanie.

Stephanie glanced at Allie. She expected her to say I told you so.

Instead, Allie frowned at her in concern. "How do you feel now?" she asked.

"Better," Stephanie admitted, lifting her head. "Are they still there?"

Maura stepped out of the doorway and checked. "No. They left. I think they went up to the food court."

"Does either of you know that girl?" Stephanie asked.

Maura and Allie both shook their heads.

"This is unbelievable," Allie said. "Here you lost one of your best friends over Alex—and he's out with someone else!"

"He wasn't serious about me at all," Stephanie murmured. "I wish I'd listened to you before, Allie," she said.

"I'm kind of sorry I was right about him," Allie told her. "I never wanted this to happen, Steph."

"Me, either," Stephanie replied. "I'm just glad

you both saw him, too. Or I wouldn't have believed my own eyes."

"We saw it, all right," Maura remarked. "He sure had me fooled."

"You, and me, and Darcy," Allie added.

Stephanie shook her head. She didn't know what to do now. "Do you guys mind if I don't see the movie?" she asked. "I think I need to go home and think."

"Sure. We understand," Allie replied. "We'll drop you off. I don't feel like a movie, either."

"Thanks," Stephanie said. "You're really good friends."

"Great news!" Michelle cried as Stephanie flung open the front door. "And I owe it all to you!"

Stephanie glanced at Michelle. She was in no mood to talk to anyone. But Michelle was positively beaming with happiness.

"What is it, Michelle?" she asked.

"Ms. Yoshida said my photo essay was the best in the whole class!" Michelle was bursting with pride. "She said it had a dynamic story line."

"What did she mean by that?" Stephanie asked.

"She said I captured the action of a blossoming romance," Michelle explained. "Boy, Steph, stealing Darcy's boyfriend was a great idea. At least for my project," she added.

Stephanie's eyes filled with tears. "Except I didn't get a boyfriend," she said. "I just caught a rat."

D.J. looked up from the couch. "Stephanie, what's the matter?" she demanded.

"Everything!" Stephanie collapsed onto the couch next to D.J. She explained about catching Alex kissing another girl.

"That must have been horrible for you," D.J. commented.

"Alex is a lying creep," Michelle declared.

"But he didn't lie. Not really," Stephanie said, wiping the tears out of her eyes. "He never said I was his only girlfriend."

"He led you to believe it, though," D.J. disagreed. "He acted like he was interested only in you."

"That's the same as lying, isn't it?" Michelle asked.

"I think so," D.J. replied. "When a guy acts like he's wild about you, you assume you're the only one he's dating."

"That's the way I thought it was," Stephanie admitted. "Now I feel like an idiot. I actually thought it was true love or something." She considered. "I wonder if that's what Darcy thought, too!"

Mentioning Darcy made her feel a sudden burst of anger.

She'd hurt Darcy, and for what? Nothing!

"I can't believe I sacrificed one of my best friends for a guy who turned out to be a liar!" she exclaimed.

"You should really let him have it," D.J. declared.

"That's what I plan to do," Stephanie replied. "I'm going to break up with him before he has a chance to break up with me."

"Good for you," D.J. declared. "But what about Darcy?"

"I don't know," Stephanie admitted. Breaking up with Alex was the easy part. But making up with Darcy—that was going to be the really hard part.

CHAPTER
15

◆ ◄ ◆ ◆

"Good news!" Allie declared in excitement. She stopped by Stephanie's locker just as Stephanie slammed the door shut.

"Let me guess," Stephanie replied. "Alex was abducted by aliens last night."

Allie rolled her eyes. "Not that good," she said. "No. The good news is, I spoke to Darcy last night. She doesn't blame Maura and me anymore. She realizes we were caught in the middle."

"But she still hates me, doesn't she?" Stephanie said.

Allie nodded. "Sorry. I tried to explain your side of it. But she wouldn't listen."

"Did you tell her about last night?" Stephanie asked.

"I just couldn't," Allie admitted. "I didn't know how to explain it."

"I don't think I'd know how to say it, either," Stephanie agreed. "I still can't believe I saw what I saw."

"But you did," Allie confirmed. "We all did."

"I know." Stephanie sighed. "That's the rotten thing."

"How are you doing today?" Allie asked. "Any better?"

"Actually, I feel more angry than sad today," Stephanie said as they headed down the hall toward homeroom.

"I don't blame you," Allie told her.

"Allie, you never once said 'I told you so,'" Stephanie pointed out. "Even though you didn't like Alex from the start. I want you to know I think that's really cool."

Allie smiled. "Thanks," she said.

They continued down the hall. They turned a corner and stopped short.

Alex!

He leaned against a locker, laughing. Stephanie's eyes narrowed as she recognized the redheaded girl from last night. The girl he'd been kissing at the mall!

Allie gasped. Stephanie nodded to her grimly. Together, they ducked back around the corner.

"I can't believe it!" Allie exclaimed. "It's her! The girl from the movies."

"She must be in seventh grade," Stephanie said in a low voice. "That's why we never noticed her before."

"Or she could be new, or a transfer student," Allie added.

Stephanie covered her mouth with her hand, signaling for Allie to keep quiet. She leaned around the corner.

Alex and the girl were still there.

Neither of them noticed her. They couldn't see her, but she could hear them clearly.

"Hey, want to go to the movie they're showing in the cafeteria tonight?" Alex asked.

"Okay," the girl agreed. "I'll meet you here. Hey, I want to tell you a joke I just heard . . ."

Stephanie felt a sharp jab in the ribs. She glanced up. Allie was pointing at someone passing in the hall. Darcy!

"She's going to see Alex," Allie declared.

Stephanie's mind raced. What should she do?

Should she save Darcy from a horrible surprise? And especially on her birthday.

There was no time to decide. In the next second, Darcy would turn the corner.

"Darcy!" Stephanie called in a sharp whisper.

Darcy turned toward her with a surprised expression. Her eyes clouded when she realized Stephanie had called. "What do you want?" she snapped.

"You've got to come here." Stephanie waved her over.

"Before you see something awful," Allie added.

Darcy glared at Stephanie but joined Allie. "What is it?" she asked.

"Around the corner," Allie told her. "It's Alex."

Darcy blinked, then poked her head around the corner.

"Meredith, you are too much," Alex said, laughing over Meredith's joke. "So, what time do you want me to meet you tonight?"

"Seven is good," Meredith answered.

"Great! It's a date." Alex reached out and gave her a quick hug.

Meredith shut her locker. Alex's voice grew faint as they walked off together down the hall.

Darcy stared at Stephanie, wide-eyed with confusion. "I don't get it," she said. "He's going out with *her*, too?"

Stephanie nodded slowly. "And we saw him kissing her at the mall yesterday."

Darcy frowned. "Well, he's just kissing *everybody* these days, isn't he?"

"Just about," Allie agreed.

Darcy gazed hard at Stephanie. "It looks like he fooled us both, doesn't it?" she said.

"He got us good," Stephanie agreed.

"I'm going to tell him exactly what I think of him!" Darcy's eyes flashed with anger. "Right here and—"

Stephanie grabbed her wrist. "Wait. We can do better than that if you can spend your birthday with me tonight."

"What do you mean?" Darcy asked.

Stephanie grinned mischievously at the idea forming in her mind. "Did Alex ever officially break up with you?" she asked.

"No," Darcy realized. "But then, we haven't talked much at all since . . . well, you know." Darcy's cheeks flushed.

"That's what I thought," Stephanie said. "So, as far as Alex knows, you must still consider yourself his girlfriend."

Darcy nodded thoughtfully. "Right. So what?"

"So he hasn't broken up with me, either," Stephanie pointed out. "And that means we both might be pretty upset to catch him with another girl."

"I don't see your point," Darcy said.

"You will—after we work out all the details of my plan—and rock that big rat's world," Stephanie finished.

"All right, I get it," Darcy said. "But just remember, we're not friends. I'm still really mad at you."

"Okay," Stephanie agreed. "So this is what I have in mind . . ."

Stephanie squirmed uncomfortably on the metal folding chair. The darkened cafeteria was packed. The movie being shown that evening was the popular old mystery thriller *Rear Window*. Tons of kids came to watch.

Normally, she would have found it pretty interesting herself. But tonight she couldn't keep her mind on a movie. All she could think about was Alex. She stole another glance at him, sitting with his arm around Meredith's shoulder ten rows away.

She glanced at Darcy, who sat on the other side of the room. They had sneaked in together after the lights were already dimmed. They chose to split up, deciding that their plan would be more effective if they didn't sit together.

What they were about to do might upset Meredith, Stephanie realized. But in the end, she and Darcy were doing Meredith a favor. Alex was sure to treat her badly someday, just as badly as he'd treated Stephanie and Darcy. Meredith might as well find out what a rat he was sooner rather than later.

Finally, after what seemed like forever, the closing movie credits began to roll. Stephanie drew in a deep breath. This was it. Show time!

The cafeteria lights came up. There was a burst of talk and laughter as the crowd began moving out of their seats. Darcy and Stephanie exchanged a quick glance. Then they both headed up the aisle—right in Alex's direction.

Darcy reached Alex a split second before she did.

"Alex! Sweetie!" Darcy exclaimed, reaching for Alex's left arm.

Stephanie quickly grabbed his right arm. "Alex, honey! Here you are!"

Alex looked startled. Then horrified.

Stephanie laughed at his shocked expression.

"Hey, why are you hanging on my boyfriend's arm?" Darcy demanded of Stephanie. Her voice was so loud that the kids nearby stopped to see what was happening.

"*Your* boyfriend!" Stephanie cried, as if she were outraged. "Alex is *my* boyfriend now. Alex," she demanded, "didn't you tell her about us?"

Alex's eyes widened in panic. "I, uh . . . wh-what?" he blurted out.

"Alex, tell her you like me," Darcy said.

"No, he likes me! And I have a picture to prove it right here!" Stephanie pulled Michelle's crumpled photo from her pocket and held it up so that everyone—especially Meredith—could take a good, long look.

Meredith stared at the photo. She stepped away from Alex. "You didn't tell me you had other girl-friends," she said. "What a creep!"

"And a liar," a girl nearby commented.

"Oh, he's a *big* liar," Stephanie agreed. "He actually thought he could go out with my best friend, and me, and now Meredith—without any of us finding out!"

"That stinks," someone else murmured.

Alex had recovered from his shock. He flashed his most charming smile and shrugged. "What can I say? Girls like me. And I like girls. What's wrong with that?" he asked.

"What's wrong is that girls happen to like honesty, and truthfulness, and loyalty," Darcy calmly replied.

"I guess those things are unimportant to you," Stephanie suggested.

"Okay, you're mad," Alex said. "Then don't go out with me anymore."

Darcy snorted. "Don't worry about that," she said.

"Really," Stephanie agreed. "By tomorrow morning, every girl in this school will know about you. I don't think anyone will want to go out with you again."

"Yeah," a girl standing beside her added. "You'd better transfer to another school if you want another girlfriend."

"As if I need another girlfriend," Alex bragged. "I have Meredith. She's the only one I want." He stepped toward her, but Meredith turned her back and walked away.

Alex stood alone for a moment. Then he shrugged and marched out of the auditorium, pretending not to notice everyone staring at him.

Stephanie glanced at Darcy. The sparkle in Darcy's eyes set her off. Both of them screamed with laughter. The kids standing nearest them began laughing along.

Darcy held her sides as she tried to catch her breath. "That was great, Stephanie. The best birthday present ever," she said. "It was so great that I almost forgot something important!"

"What's that?" Stephanie asked.

Darcy's laughter faded. "I almost forgot that I'm still mad at you."

CHAPTER
16

◆ ◀ ✦ ◆

Stephanie leaned across the booth at Luigi's Pizzeria the next day after school. Darcy sat opposite her.

"I felt the worst that you would betray me like that," Darcy was saying. "That bothered me more than losing Alex."

"I know what you mean," Stephanie told her. "I thought I liked Alex so much! I was totally destroyed when I saw him kissing Meredith. But after a while I realized I was also more upset about losing your friendship than about losing him."

"But if you hadn't caught him, you'd still be

going out with him, wouldn't you?" Darcy asked.

"I'm not sure," Stephanie admitted. "I guess I'll never know for sure. I hope we can be friends again, though."

Darcy's serious expression turned into a grin. "Only if you promise to never let a boy come between us again."

"Done," Stephanie declared. "And if we ever like the *same* guy, we'll talk about it. Openly. Deal?"

"Deal," Darcy agreed, reaching across the table to squeeze Stephanie's hand.

"Is it safe to sit down now?" Allie appeared at their booth with Maura by her side.

"Totally safe," Stephanie replied.

Allie and Maura slid in.

"You know, you guys, we have some unfinished business to attend to," Darcy said. "Now that we're all friends again, what are you planning for my birthday?"

"Birthday?" Allie asked, looking innocent.

"She's teasing," Stephanie said. "I told Darcy all about the surprise party. I had to— to explain how everything happened with Alex."

Allie turned to Darcy. "Would you still like to have one?" she asked. "You can pretend to be surprised."

"Definitely!" Darcy squealed.

"Way to go!" Stephanie cheered. "It's party time!"

"Smile, everybody!" Michelle's camera flash lit up the Tanner living room on Saturday night.

Stephanie gave her a thumbs-up. Hiring Michelle to be official party photographer was a brilliant idea. Michelle was happy to come to the party. And Stephanie was happy to get great shots of all her friends.

"Everything is going great," Allie observed.

"Yup. The kids are having a terrific time," Stephanie agreed, glancing at couples talking and dancing.

"That's not what I mean," Allie replied. "Look who Darcy is talking to."

Stephanie sighted Darcy across the room. She was deep in conversation with Ben.

"She's actually smiling at him," Allie noted, pleased.

"At least she's giving him a chance," Stephanie agreed.

Allie gave her a long look. "Hey! Why don't you mingle more, Steph? This would be a good chance for you to meet someone new. Have you met Spencer's friend Tyler? "

"No thanks!" Stephanie shook her head. "I think I'll take a break from boys for a while. It's nice to be on my own for now."

"I suppose so," Allie said. She turned her head. "Hey, there's Meredith!" she exclaimed in surprise. "I didn't know she was coming."

Stephanie waved as Meredith crossed the living room. "Yeah, I called her at the last minute. I figured she might be going through a bad time, too. Now that she knows the truth about Alex."

"That was nice of you," Allie commented.

"It was the least I could do," Stephanie replied.

Darcy wove her way through the crowd to join them. "This is the best party, you guys. Thanks." She hugged Stephanie and Allie. "It's a great birthday present."

Stephanie grinned. "That's all we wanted to hear."

"So—did Ben ask you out?" Allie asked Darcy.

"No. But you're right. He's really nice," Darcy replied.

Allie frowned. "I'm going to find Spencer," she declared.

"Why? What's wrong?" Darcy asked.

"He needs to talk to Ben about being too shy," Allie declared, leaving them.

Darcy burst out laughing. So did Stephanie.

"Allie needs to learn the lesson we learned," Stephanie said. "You can't make a boy any different than the way he is."

"That's the truth!" Darcy declared. "You know, Steph, I owe you an apology."

"For what?" Stephanie asked.

"Allie told me that Alex forgot my birthday until you reminded him," Darcy replied. "I would have been home alone this weekend, feeling miserable and let down. Instead, I'm having a blast."

Stephanie gave Darcy a giant hug. "It is a good party, isn't it?"

"The best," Darcy said, hugging back. "Because I'm sharing it with my best friends. And that's the best birthday present of all."

FULL HOUSE™

SISTERS

A brand-new series starring Stephanie AND Michelle!

#1 Two On The Town

Stephanie and Michelle find themselves
in the big city—and in big trouble!

#2 One Boss Too Many

Stephanie and Michelle think camp will be major fun.
If only these two sisters were getting along!

When sisters get together...expect the unexpected!

A MINSTREL® BOOK

Published by Pocket Books

2012-01

FULL HOUSE Stephanie™

PHONE CALL FROM A FLAMINGO	88004-7/$3.99
THE BOY-OH-BOY NEXT DOOR	88121-3/$3.99
TWIN TROUBLES	88290-2/$3.99
HIP HOP TILL YOU DROP	88291-0/$3.99
HERE COMES THE BRAND NEW ME	89858-2/$3.99
THE SECRET'S OUT	89859-0/$3.99
DADDY'S NOT-SO-LITTLE GIRL	89860-4/$3.99
P.S. FRIENDS FOREVER	89861-2/$3.99
GETTING EVEN WITH THE FLAMINGOES	52273-6/$3.99
THE DUDE OF MY DREAMS	52274-4/$3.99
BACK-TO-SCHOOL COOL	52275-2/$3.99
PICTURE ME FAMOUS	52276-0/$3.99
TWO-FOR-ONE CHRISTMAS FUN	53546-3/$3.99
THE BIG FIX-UP MIX-UP	53547-1/$3.99
TEN WAYS TO WRECK A DATE	53548-X/$3.99
WISH UPON A VCR	53549-8/$3.99
DOUBLES OR NOTHING	56841-8/$3.99
SUGAR AND SPICE ADVICE	56842-6/$3.99
NEVER TRUST A FLAMINGO	56843-4/$3.99
THE TRUTH ABOUT BOYS	00361-5/$3.99
CRAZY ABOUT THE FUTURE	00362-3/$3.99
MY SECRET ADMIRER	00363-1/$3.99
BLUE RIBBON CHRISTMAS	00830-7/$3.99
THE STORY ON OLDER BOYS	00831-5/$3.99
MY THREE WEEKS AS A SPY	00832-3/$3.99
NO BUSINESS LIKE SHOW BUSINESS	01725-X/$3.99
MAIL-ORDER BROTHER	01726-8/$3.99
TO CHEAT OR NOT TO CHEAT	01727-6/$3.99
WINNING IS EVERYTHING	02098-6/$3.99
HELLO BIRTHDAY, GOOD-BYE FRIEND	02160-5/$3.99

Available from Minstrel® Books Published by Pocket Books

Simon & Schuster Mail Order Dept. BWB
200 Old Tappan Rd., Old Tappan, N.J. 07675

Please send me the books I have checked above. I am enclosing $_____(please add $0.75 to cover the postage and handling for each order. Please add appropriate sales tax). Send check or money order--no cash or C.O.D.'s please. Allow up to six weeks for delivery. For purchase over $10.00 you may use VISA: card number, expiration date and customer signature must be included.

Name _____

Address _____

City _____ State/Zip _____

VISA Card # _____ Exp.Date _____

Signature _____

TM & © 1998 Warner Bros. All Right Reserved.

929-26

FULL HOUSE™
Michelle

#5: THE GHOST IN MY CLOSET 53573-0/$3.99
#6: BALLET SURPRISE 53574-9/$3.99
#7: MAJOR LEAGUE TROUBLE 53575-7/$3.99
#8: MY FOURTH-GRADE MESS 53576-5/$3.99
#9: BUNK 3, TEDDY, AND ME 56834-5/$3.99
#10: MY BEST FRIEND IS A MOVIE STAR!
(Super Edition) 56835-3/$3.99
#11: THE BIG TURKEY ESCAPE 56836-1/$3.99
#12: THE SUBSTITUTE TEACHER 00364-X/$3.99
#13: CALLING ALL PLANETS 00365-8/$3.99
#14: I'VE GOT A SECRET 00366-6/$3.99
#15: HOW TO BE COOL 00833-1/$3.99
#16: THE NOT-SO-GREAT OUTDOORS 00835-8/$3.99
#17: MY HO-HO-HORRIBLE CHRISTMAS 00836-6/$3.99
MY AWESOME HOLIDAY FRIENDSHIP BOOK
(An Activity Book) 00840-4/$3.99
FULL HOUSE MICHELLE OMNIBUS 02181-8/$6.99
#18: MY ALMOST PERFECT PLAN 00837-4/$3.99
#19: APRIL FOOLS 01729-2/$3.99
#20: MY LIFE IS A THREE-RING CIRCUS 01730-6/$3.99
#21: WELCOME TO MY ZOO 01731-4/$3.99
#22: THE PROBLEM WITH PEN PALS 01732-2/$3.99
#23: MERRY CHRISTMAS, WORLD! 02098-6/$3.99
#24: TAP DANCE TROUBLE 02154-0/$3.99
MY SUPER SLEEPOVER BOOK 02701-8/$3.99

A MINSTREL® BOOK   Published by Pocket Books

Simon & Schuster Mail Order Dept. BWB
200 Old Tappan Rd., Old Tappan, N.J. 07675

Please send me the books I have checked above. I am enclosing $_____ (please add $0.75 to cover the
postage and handling for each order. Please add appropriate sales tax). Send check or money order--no cash or C.O.D.'s please. Allow up to
six weeks for delivery. For purchase over $10.00 you may use VISA: card number, expiration date and customer signature must be included.

Name _____

Address _____

City _____ State/Zip _____

VISA Card # _____ Exp.Date _____

Signature _____

™ & © 1997 Warner Bros. All Rights Reserved.

1033-29